# "Becker?" Faith whispered, trying to suppress a gasp

as a well-built guy emerged from the bathroom wearing only a white towel wrapped around his waist.

Faith's eyes hung on his muscular physique. It seemed impossible that this was the same bookish guy in the baggy clothes she'd met yesterday.

"Hi," Becker said lightly as Faith opened the door for him. "How did you sleep?"

"Uh, fine," Faith managed, turning and flattening up against the door as he passed. She was unable to take her eyes off him. Becker's wet, dark hair was neatly slicked back. Yesterday, it had covered half his face. This morning, she could see the strong bones in his face and his high, smooth brow. Becker Cain wasn't just a good-looking guy. He was gorgeous. And he was sharing Faith's dorm room for a whole week.

Don't miss these books
in the exciting FRESHMAN DORM series

*Freshman Dorm*
*Freshman Lies*
*Freshman Guys*
*Freshman Nights*
*Freshman Dreams*
*Freshman Games*
*Freshman Loves*
*Freshman Secrets*
*Freshman Schemes*
*Freshman Changes*
*Freshman Fling*
*Freshman Rivals*
*Freshman Heartbreak*
*Freshman Flames*
*Freshman Choices*
*Freshman Feud*
*Freshman Follies*
*Freshman Wedding*
*Freshman Promises*
*Freshman Summer*
*Freshman Affair*
*Freshman Truths*
*Freshman Scandal*
*Freshman Christmas*

And, coming soon . . .

*Freshman Obsession*

# FRESHMAN ROOMMATE

LINDA A. COONEY

HarperPaperbacks
*A Division of* HarperCollins*Publishers*

This is a work of fiction. The characters, incidents, and dialogues are products of the author's imagination and are not to be construed as real. Any resemblance to actual events or persons, living or dead, is entirely coincidental.

HarperPaperbacks   *A Division of* HarperCollins*Publishers*
10 East 53rd Street, New York, N.Y. 10022

Cover illustration by Tony Greco

First printing: January 1993

Printed in the United States of America

HarperPaperbacks and colophon are trademarks of HarperCollins*Publishers*

❖ 10 9 8 7 6 5 4 3 2 1

# One

．．．．．．．．．．

**F**aith Crowley slammed her history book shut, sat cross-legged on her bed, and closed her eyes.

"Niccolò Machiavelli," she recited, "fourteen sixty-nine to fifteen twenty-seven. Italian statesman and political philosopher. Best known for his work *The Prince*, which earned him his reputation as a teacher of treachery, intrigue, and immorality."

The afternoon sun slanted through the window of Faith's Coleridge Hall dorm room as she and two of her best friends crammed for a Western Civ exam. Scattered around the room were study notes, highlighter pens, and empty chip bags.

Lauren Turnbell-Smythe glanced up from her notebook, narrowed her violet eyes, and leaned back against the edge of Faith's bed. "Machiavelli. Typical male," she declared, pushing her wire-rimmed glasses up on her nose. "Sounds like men haven't changed much in five hundred years."

"Give me a break," said Winnie Gottlieb, one of Faith's best friends from high school. Winnie looked more petite than usual in her oversized man's undershirt and glittery purple tights. Her spiky brown hair poked out all around her head. "If anyone's qualified to comment on men, it's me. After all, I'm the one who's married."

"Ouch," Lauren teased. "You don't exactly sound like the radiant bride today. Are you going to share it with us, or brood about it all day?"

"Brood," Winnie said, her dark eyes moving sullenly from Lauren to Faith. "That is—until my friend Faith here agrees to stop studying and talk to me."

Faith dug her hand into a bowl of popcorn and looked thoughtfully at Winnie. Hyper, brilliant Winnie had been her best friend since junior high. Faith knew the warning signs of all of Winnie's moods. Right now Faith recognized Winnie's I'm-so-depressed-that-I'm-not-going-to-say-anything-until-someone-cares-enough-to-drag-it-out-of-me routine.

Faith let out a long sigh. She had always been there

for Winnie—to help her up when she was down, and to bring her down to earth when she was about to go out of control.

But this week was different, Faith thought, nervously rubbing the tops of her soft jeans with her palms. For once, Mother Faith was going to have to shut down her confessional box. For once, Winnie was going to have to survive without her.

This week Faith had something to do that was more important than anything she'd ever done.

Leaning back against her pillow and stretching out her long legs, Faith smiled as she thought about the dream she'd been waiting for all her life to come true. And now it was right before her, within her grasp.

The U. of S. Professional Theater Program. Just thinking about it sent shivers of terror and excitement up and down Faith's spine. The Program. As in: one of the country's top training programs for future stage directors, producers, actors, and playwrights.

The Program. As in: small, elite classes on specialized topics with students who were as dedicated to the theater as she was.

The Program. As in: seminars with theater heavies from around the country, more opportunities to direct, better access to the university stage.

Faith sprang up from the bed and began to pace

the room, wringing her hands. The only trouble was, the timing couldn't have been worse. The interview for the program was an oral presentation before the entire drama faculty this coming Friday. Her assignment was to develop an original production idea for *The Taming of the Shrew.*

Everything depended on how creative her idea was and how well she presented it. But the presentation was the day after her monster Western Civ exam. If she didn't plan her week down to the very second, she could blow everything.

Her GPA.

And her entire future in the theater.

"Stop pacing, Faith," Lauren said impatiently. "The exam counts for half our grade, but it's not going to be *that* bad. Plus, if you're not going to study, let's talk. There's something I really need to get off my chest."

Faith stopped pacing, irritated. The room suddenly felt small and she wondered if it had been a good idea to invite her two friends over for the cramming session. They always ended up talking about their personal problems. "It's not just the exam, Lauren."

"What?" Winnie looked up and snapped a large purple bubble of gum.

Faith sighed. "I told you guys. Don't you remember? The Professional Theater Program. On Friday, I've got to get up on stage before the entire drama department faculty and present a brilliant *Taming of the Shrew* concept."

"Sexist garbage," Lauren sneered. "I don't care if it's Shakespeare. The story is about a bunch of guys who want to tame the only woman with guts in the town."

Faith glared at her. "Okay. So you know the story. But it doesn't have to play that way. Shakespeare's language is so rich, there are usually a hundred different ways to interpret a scene or a relationship or a . . ."

"I thought we were studying Western Civ, not British Lit," Winnie complained. She yawned and patted her mouth with her glossy orange nails.

"But, Lauren," Faith persisted, ignoring Winnie. "Don't you see? The story could take place anywhere. The whole point of the program's entrance exam is to show the drama faculty that you can give it new meaning simply by changing the context. It doesn't have to take place in Elizabethan England. It could be in a twentieth-century suburb. Or a circus. Or maybe during the New England witch trials. The important thing is to make it come alive. Make the audience look at it in a fresh way."

Faith looked down. Winnie had stretched out on the floor and, using her textbook as a pillow, had dozed off. Lauren was giggling. Faith shook her head. "Thanks, you guys. Forget it. I'll handle this problem myself."

Lauren laughed softly. "Oh well, at least your noisy roommate Liza is gone for the week. You'll have some peace and quiet for a change. Then you'll be able to think."

Faith's mouth dropped open. "I just remembered something."

Lauren narrowed her eyes. "Oh, no. Liza left her favorite feather boa behind and she's on her way to retrieve it?"

Faith shook her head, feeling more agitated by the second. "It was probably a big mistake, but I signed up for that Coed-by-Bed experiment. And now I'm stuck with it, even though this is just about the worst week of my life. The guy's supposed to show up today."

"Coed-by-Bed?" Lauren snickered. "How could you do this to yourself?"

Faith gave Lauren a weary look. She had the impulse to get a broom and sweep everyone and everything out of her room. Instead, she tried to stay calm. These were her good friends, after all. It wasn't their fault that she had the busiest week of her life. "The whole idea, *Lauren*, is to see if you can live with a guy for a week on a purely nonromantic basis."

Winnie's eyes opened wide. "Impossible."

"It's supposed to promote better understanding between the sexes," Faith explained, fiddling with the metal spiral on her notebook and wondering how she always managed to make her life more complicated than anyone else's. "His name is Becker Cain and he's from the all-male study dorm. I think he's a sophomore."

"He's probably in the dorm experiment to impress his friends," Lauren said, giggling. "And to meet some freshman women."

"Yeah, so don't go and sleep with him!" Winnie yelled, sitting up and laughing hysterically, as Lauren noisily blew up an empty chip bag and punched it victoriously.

Something caught Faith's eye. She looked up and drew her breath in sharply. Standing in the doorway was a tall guy wearing an oversize dark coat, a black T-shirt, and dark baggy pants over a pair of high-top sneakers. A white button with a large black question mark on it was pinned to his lapel.

"Faith Crowley?" he asked in a polite tone, not moving.

"Yes?" Faith stared at him. There was something cool and detached in his intelligent blue eyes. His face was long and well shaped, as if someone had chiseled the deep cleft in his chin and smoothed his brow up to his dark hairline. Framing his perfect features was long, dark-brown hair, parted on the side. For a moment, Faith had the feeling his blue eyes were looking deep into her soul. A shiver went through her. Was he a stranger, or someone she'd met before?

"I'm Becker Cain," the guy said tentatively. Then a warm grin spread across his face and his eyes crinkled with humor. "Remember? The dorm experiment?"

Faith shook her head to bring herself back to the present. "Oh! Yes! Becker. Um . . . Hi." Faith walked shyly toward him, desperately hoping he hadn't caught Winnie's loud remark about sleeping together. "Hi."

"Hi." Becker stood there, staring at Faith, while Faith stared back. Then he looked shyly down at Lauren and Winnie, still sprawled on the floor.

Winnie sat up straight and gave Becker a huge grin. "Don't mind us. We're just here to drive Faith around the bend while she's trying to study. It's our purpose in life, you see."

Becker looked politely at Winnie as if she were from another planet.

Lauren leaned back on the bed and gave him a challenging look. "After all, what are friends for?"

Becker turned, then gave Lauren a friendly smile. Faith noticed that his teeth were very white and straight. "'The only way to have a friend is to be one.' Do you know it?" Becker asked cheerfully. "Ralph Waldo Emerson. Nineteenth-century American philosopher."

Lauren looked heavenward as Winnie groaned in

the background. Faith's eyes opened wide as she watched Lauren and Becker stare each other down.

"What's that supposed to mean?" Lauren asked, rising to her feet.

"Well," Becker began patiently. "I guess it means that if your friend wants to study, she should be able to." He stepped around the piles of junk on the floor and set down his duffel and a large book bag on Liza's bed. Then he brushed a strand of hair back behind his ear and sat down.

There was a long silence. Faith sat down carefully on her bed and twirled her braid around her finger. She looked at Becker, then glanced uncomfortably at Lauren, who looked as if she were going to deliver one of her self-defense class kicks to Becker's midsection. Instead, Lauren began stuffing her notes in her book bag. Winnie slammed her book shut and huffed, "Okay, Faith. We'll leave. You and Mr. Transcendentalist need time to get to know each other."

"Hey, I'm sorry," Becker apologized. "I didn't mean to break this up."

Winnie returned Becker's gaze with an even stare, then gave Faith a pleading look over her shoulder as she headed to the door. "We still need to talk," she said. "Call me."

"Okay. I will. Thanks, you guys," Faith called weakly as the door shut with a hollow thud.

Suddenly the room was unbearably quiet.

Faith squirmed. Outside in the hall she could hear the familiar sounds of music and singing that were all part of the creative arts dorm. The voices of an a cappella group singing down on the green drifted up through the window. The ticking of her alarm clock became irritatingly loud. She slid her eyes nervously across the room toward Becker and strained to smile. *This is unbelievable,* she thought. *First the exam. Then the drama presentation. Then my overdependent friends. And now a completely strange guy living four feet away from me all week. Can I handle this?*

"Did I say the wrong thing?" Becker asked softly. His clear blue eyes were fringed with dark lashes. He had a narrow, aristocratic nose and pale, translucent skin. But his lips were very full and expressive.

"Um, no," Faith said. She wondered how long she was going to have to make conversation before she could gracefully get back to work. "They're just my friends."

Becker stood up and cast a curious look around the room. He took off his jacket, revealing a pair of wide, muscular shoulders. Faith was surprised. *Guys with great builds usually didn't wear black and lug heavy book bags,* she thought. They were usually jocks who wore rugby shirts and track shorts. Becker seemed different. Very different.

Becker opened his duffel bag and unpacked a few

things in silence. He finally sat down, crossed his long legs, and slid one arm back along the bed's backrest. "Your friends," he repeated.

"Yup." Faith cleared her throat anxiously, slipped her elbow out to the side, and spilled a whole can of soda on her desk. Jumping up, she looked around desperately for something to keep it from soaking into a pile of books.

"Whoops." Becker leaped to the rescue, grabbing one of his hand towels on the way.

"Oh," Faith mumbled, feeling desperately awkward and trapped. "Oh, thanks. I, um . . ."

"You were about to tell me about your friends," Becker prompted, calmly draping the towel on a closet doorknob.

"Yeah," Faith continued. "I'm surrounded by them. They lurk behind doors and spring out at me from dark corners. Old friends. New friends. Theater friends. Dorm friends. Even friends who aren't here, like my roommate. But I guess that's why you're here—"

Faith stopped herself when she realized Becker was looking at her with amusement. "I've always found that one good friend is all you need," he said.

"Really? Interesting concept."

A smile played at the corners of his mouth. He took out a shower kit. Faith smelled a vaguely familiar after-shave scent. "I become distracted, unfocused, and slightly psychotic when I'm surrounded by well-meaning friends and family," she said.

She leaned back on her bed and drew up her knees, feeling a bit more relaxed. Becker seemed to understand her current situation, which was more than she could say for Lauren and Winnie. "I think I know what you mean about having only one good friend."

"I could tell."

There was another long silence as Faith watched Becker, wondering what to say next as he carefully arranged his belongings. She *wanted* to talk to him a little more. But her panicky feeling returned.

"So," she began purposefully, standing up, "you'll understand when I tell you that this week is shaping up into a monster. I don't know how much time I'll have to get to know you."

Becker gave Faith a serene look as he unbuckled his study book bag. He stood up and began unloading books onto Liza's desk, placing them in neat stacks. "I can tell this is going to work out just fine, then."

"You can?" Faith's muscles relaxed a little.

Becker inspected the bottom of his book bag and pulled out several neatly bound notebooks. "I'm a philosophy major in Honor's College. I need at least four hours per day to get through the reading requirements alone."

"Wow," Faith whispered, beginning to feel a little guilty for making such a big deal about her Western

Civ exam. With Becker as a roommate, studying would be no problem at all. In fact, she'd get much more done with Becker than she would have with Liza. Liza couldn't enter a room without turning it upside down and doubling the noise level.

"I'm used to a quiet environment and I don't have time to drink or party. For relaxation, I meditate daily. And I don't smoke or eat meat."

"Sounds good to me."

"About your privacy," Becker said matter-of-factly as he lifted a stack of T-shirts. "Don't worry about me. If I'm here when you need to change clothes, just tell me to close my eyes. And I'll also try to let the women in the hall know when I'm using the bathroom."

Faith grinned. "Are you always this . . . um . . . organized?"

Becker was refolding a T-shirt. "I try to be," he murmured. Then he shrugged. "I know it seems a little absurd sometimes. But it's just the way I am. I don't deal with chaos too well. So I try to avoid it."

A smile played at the corner of Faith's mouth. At last, here was someone who could tell her how to avoid chaos. Had they been paired up by a computer or a divine spirit? "Tell me something," Faith blurted. "Why did you sign up for this experiment?"

Becker turned around and looked at Faith thoughtfully. He climbed up on Liza's desk, crossed his legs, and cradled his chin in his hand. "I think routine and discipline are good," Becker said slowly. "But I also believe in change. Imagination thrives on the unexpected. On adventure. Surprise." He pointed good-naturedly to the button on his lapel. "Questions."

Faith smiled and slipped her hands in her jean pockets, self-conscious again. "I wish I could give you an explanation that was as thoughtful, but I'm kind of brain-dead this week."

Becker shrugged. "But that's what's so amazing about the mind."

"What?"

"It has the power to renew itself."

"Oh good," Faith joked, settling back down on her bed with her Western Civ notes.

"So I'll just let you go ahead and recharge, okay?" Becker concluded, reaching for a book and turning on Liza's reading lamp.

"Okay," Faith said quietly. She gazed out over the newly ordered vista. After only a few minutes with Becker, she felt more relaxed and appreciated than she had for months with her best friends.

So far, this experiment was turning out great.

Faith didn't know Becker at all. But she knew she agreed with him on one major point.

She believed in change, too.

# Two

The stewardess spoke briskly into the microphone. "On behalf of Trans-Western Airlines, I'd like to welcome you to the Los Angeles International Airport. Please stay in your seats until the plane has come to a complete stop."

*I will never come to a complete stop,* Liza Ruff thought with joy as the huge plane rumbled toward the gate. She dug into her purse, pulled out her rhinestone-studded compact, and grinned at her reflection in the tiny mirror.

Here she was, a million miles from Brooklyn, inches away from Hollywood, and only hours away from the screen test that was sure to launch her spectacular career. From now on, the world was going to be at her feet.

Liza sighed and began to dab her nose with powder. Not a perfect face. Maybe a little chubby. Maybe almost pretty. "But look at where it got me," she muttered.

Only a short time ago she'd been a mere freshman at the University of Springfield. She dutifully attended her drama classes. She got small parts in plays at the university theater. Everything in her life was about as ordinary as her mom's Brooklyn-style pastrami sandwiches.

And then the *Stand Up On Campus* comedy contest came along.

Suddenly, she was out on the stage, cracking the same jokes she'd made up for her friends in the dorm. Except that, all of a sudden, people were actually laughing. In fact, their sides were splitting. Tears were rolling down their cheeks. Back in her Brooklyn neighborhood, everyone thought she was just like all the other wisecracking girls. In the U. of S. dorms, everyone thought she was a little bit nuts.

But on stage she was suddenly a hit.

And of course she won the contest.

The big prize? A spot on "Laugh . . . Or Else," a national cable TV show that her boyfriend Rich's Hollywood producer dad watched. And, all of a sudden, he was begging her to come for a screen test.

Because she, Liza Ruff, was apparently perfect for the lead in his new TV series, "Greasy Spoon," about a waitress in a New Jersey diner.

Liza sighed with joy.

Not only was she arriving in L.A. for a screen test, but she was actually being picked up by hot L.A. musician Travis Bennett. Thank you, Winnie Gottlieb, for calling your old pal Travis, she thought. I don't know why you're suddenly being so nice to me, but I'm not going to question it. Maybe you've seen the light about laugh-a-minute, life-of-the-party Liza Ruff.

On impulse Liza decided to rearrange her hair. Musicians liked messy hair with lots of spray, didn't they? She bent down to grab the travel bag under the seat in front of her.

"Oooh," she winced loudly as the waistband on her Lycra leggings bit into her skin. She glanced at the man sitting in the seat next to hers. "Excuse me." Liza gave him her most brilliant smile. "Can you reach that teensy-weensy little pink bag down there for me? I'm afraid I can't."

"What's the hurry?" he asked irritably, glancing briefly her way. "We're here for another fifteen minutes easy. This flight's a cattle call."

Unfazed, Liza smiled and extended her hand. "Liza Ruff. I'm in L.A. for a screen test with Bernie Greenberg. Do you know him?" Liza barely waited for an answer as the plane taxied toward the gate.

"He's practically cast me for the lead in his new television series. But he's going through the motions like he's supposed to. That's Hollywood for you."

The man looked at Liza, shook his head, then looked back down at his newspaper.

"Nice to meet you, too," Liza drawled. "Now you can say you met that big star of 'Greasy Spoon' when she first came to Hollywood, huh?"

Liza turned to gaze out at the boxy airport buildings, nearly lost in the orange-brown haze. "Smog," she whispered happily. "Real Los Angeles smog. Just like I dreamed it would look."

When it was finally time to exit the plane, Liza messed up her nest of orange-red hair a bit more and glanced confidently down at her skintight pink pants and matching sleeveless top.

Too bad all the no-sayers in the U. of S. drama department couldn't see her now. Liza was certain they'd all died of envy when she told them she was coming here to grab the lead in a hot new TV show. And they'd be singing a different tune when she returned victorious, waving her big fat contract. Maybe she'd take them all out to an expensive dinner. Just to make them feel sick for never giving her a role with more than ten lines in it.

When Liza finally emerged from the plane, the terminal was packed with tanned, hip-looking people who all seemed to know where they were going. The southern California air felt sultry and a trickle of sweat began making its way down her back. For a moment she felt her confidence waver a bit. She wasn't sure which way to go.

As she looked around the terminal, she said a small prayer. *Please, Winnie. I hope you remembered to call Travis. If I have to drop all my cash on a taxi to the Tropicana Motel right now, I'll be broke for the rest of the week. This trip is going to use up every penny I have to my name.*

Just as her head began to pound with panic, Liza caught something familiar out of the corner of her eye. She turned and almost jumped out of her skin with relief.

There, leaning against a pillar in the waiting area, was a guy with shoulder length brown hair, holding up a small sign that read: LIZA RUFF.

Liza stared for a moment in disbelief.

The guy was obviously Travis Bennett. He was supposed to pick her up, wasn't he? And there he was, carrying a sign with her name on it. Liza's heart was thumping in her chest so fast she could barely breathe. The guy was probably the best looking male in North America. Was it possible that so many wonderful things could happen at once?

"Yoo-hoo!" Liza burst out, picking up her bag. She began to run toward him, then stopped. She could see that people were looking around, as if they expected to see a rock star or a famous actress.

*Of course,* Liza realized with a jolt. *They think he's a limo driver, so they're looking to see which star he's picking up. Let's try a different approach. Stay calm for once and play the part.*

Liza planted the toes of her high-heeled sandals into the floor, straightened her back, and began to walk toward the guy with careful, slow steps. "Hello," she said, tapping him lightly on the shoulder when she reached him. "Travis, right?"

The guy's face turned her way and he smiled. Liza drew her breath in quickly. He was even better looking close up. Quickly she took in his tie-dyed T-shirt, black vest, and faded, ripped blue jeans, remembering that successful people in the entertainment industry always dressed as if they didn't have a dime.

"Hi!" Travis gave her a huge smile. "Hey. So you're Winnie's friend."

Liza stared at the way his shaggy, dark-brown hair fell around his face. His blue eyes were very intense, and sexy creases appeared at the sides of his mouth when he smiled. Winnie's friend? Hmm. Or had he been Winnie's boyfriend? Suddenly, she couldn't remember *what* Winnie had told her, except that they had met in Europe the summer before.

"I had a great flight." Liza was smiling so hard her teeth were getting dry. She prayed she didn't have lipstick on them. "Thanks for coming to meet me," she began, as they headed down the carpeted walkway, filled with kids, their harried-looking parents, and senior travelers wearing white shoes and brightly colored outfits.

"No problem," Travis said good-naturedly, staring appreciatively at her pink outfit. "When Winnie Gottlieb speaks, Travis Bennett jumps."

Liza tilted her head and wondered what he meant. From his casual tone, he sounded more like a friend than an old flame of Winnie's. But then a happy thought bubbled up inside her. What difference did it make? All she knew was that she'd finally arrived in Hollywood and she was on the arm of the cutest guy she'd ever met in her life. It was impossible to wipe the grin off her face.

She was where she belonged.

She didn't feel like a stranger here. It was almost as if she lived here her whole life. And soon, everyone would know who she was.

Liza followed Travis to the long escalator that descended to the baggage claim area. She leaned her head conspiratorially in Travis's direction. "Thanks for the little show back there, too."

Travis raised his eyebrows. "What show?"

Liza dug an elbow into his side. "You know. The limo driver act? The little sign?"

"The—limo—driver—act," Travis repeated slowly.

Liza burst into happy giggles. "Come on. I know

deadpan humor when I see it. I'm a famous comic, remember?"

Travis's face was blank. "An act?" he repeated, looking down, trying to get a glimpse of the flight numbers on the luggage carousels.

Liza threw her head back and laughed. "Ha. I love it. You crack me up, Travis."

Finally, Travis smiled a little and nodded. "Oh yeah. Limo driver. Complete with sign for the big shot arriving from first class."

"Yeah." Liza sighed. "I feel like a star already. Hey, it was cute. Thanks."

"That's half the game." Travis whistled under his breath, stuffing a hand into his jeans and stepping ahead of her on the escalator. "Act like a big star and people will treat you like one." Jumping out in front of Liza at the bottom, Travis bowed and held out his hand. "May I help you, Miss Ruff? Get you anything, Miss Ruff? Did you have a nice flight, Miss Ruff?"

Liza took his warm, strong hand and let him guide her off the escalator. "Ooooh, you know what I like, Travis Bennett."

"At your service, miss. In Winnie's honor," he said, saluting playfully. "I'll drive you anywhere you need to go. And I'll even take your many important messages on my car phone."

*"Eeeeee!"* Liza squealed, letting her eyes twinkle as

she pointed to her suitcase rumbling down the luggage carousel.

Travis swiftly grabbed the bag and smiled. "After all, isn't that why you're here? To become a big TV star?"

"Well, actually," Liza began, ecstatic that someone was listening with interest to her story. "I do have an audition tomorrow for the lead in a big new TV series. And then I'll be staying the week to meet with more important people. Apparently, I'm a shoe-in for the role." She winked at Travis. "Connections, connections. You probably know how that works."

"Oh yeah."

Liza smiled mysteriously as her high heels clicked toward the car. "Rich Greenberg. He's a guy I see at the U. of S. . . ." She looked over cautiously at Travis. "I mean, he's not my boyfriend or anything. He's just a fellow comedy nut on campus. Anyway," she continued, "Rich made his big-shot producer dad see my comedy act after I won a spot on a national cable TV show. And his dad, Bernie Greenberg, went *nuts* because he's in the middle of casting the role of 'Red' in a series about a waitress in a New Jersey diner. Well," Liza tried to catch her breath, "he absolutely insisted that I fly down immediately."

"Sounds promising." Travis nodded.

"You bet it's promising," Liza hooted, then stopped to stare with disappointment as Travis opened the trunk of a large black American-made sedan. She'd always read that successful people in the recording industry drove exotic foreign cars with convertible tops. "This is the car of a hip L.A. musician?" she blurted before she could stop herself. "Where's the convertible? Where's the zippy sportscar, pal?"

Travis looked momentarily confused, then smiled and shut the trunk with his tanned arms. He slipped on a pair of sleek dark glasses that had been hanging around his neck. "Oh, this. Well, it's the only thing big enough to carry my equipment around. Funky, huh?" He opened the door for Liza. "There's your phone."

Liza settled in the cushiony leather seat. "Yum. I like it already. It reminds me of New York, actually. And it even has tinted glass."

"Oh, yeah," Travis teased, as Liza playfully worked the automatic window button. "I wouldn't want anyone to recognize me. I'd get mobbed by the fans."

Liza made a face. Unbelievable, but true, that she could actually be making a face at this gorgeous guy. But somehow, it all fit. Travis seemed so laid back. She was beginning to feel as if she could be as crazy and carefree as she wanted—and it would still be okay.

L.A. was her kind of place. She could already tell. It was a magical town and she knew in her heart it was where she belonged. Destiny had sent her. Now she would finally be accepted—and probably even idolized—for simply being who she was.

"Okay, you heap of raw, conservative steel," Travis said as he turned on the engine. "Destination stardom."

"Destination Tropicana Motel," Liza corrected him, snapping her fingers above her head, pretending to be a Spanish dancer. She looked out the window as Travis merged into a huge freeway packed with surging traffic. "Oooh!" she squealed. "People! Cars! Civilization!"

"Danger! Ambition! Money!" Travis yelled back, instantly part of Liza's routine.

Liza screamed with laughter. A rap song blasted on the car disc player. The sun was blazing down and the cars were whizzing by and Liza just knew she was on the verge of having everything wonderful happen to her.

She shot Travis a sly look as he concentrated on passing a large truck. He was so much fun. So sweet. She couldn't remember the last time she felt this comfortable with a guy. But the fact of the matter was—guys had never been her specialty. Maybe it had something to do with her brassy red hair. Or maybe it was her big Brooklyn mouth. In any case, the only boyfriend she ever had was Rich Greenberg at the university.

But Rich was no Travis. Rich was shy, insecure, and

a little bit awkward. Travis was hip, successful, and probably rolling in money.

Plus, Liza remembered, she didn't feel guilty every time she looked at Travis. Even though she was crazy about Rich, she got terrible pangs every time she got near him. Weeks ago, during the campus comedy contest, Rich and his ventriloquist act had been her closest competition. In a white-hot moment of anger, Liza had actually stolen the dummy he needed for his act, and Rich had been forced to drop out.

After she won the contest, Rich had found out about it. But, amazingly, he had forgiven her.

Liza quickly blocked thoughts of Rich out of her mind. "So," she said, hoping she sounded like she talked to cool, handsome guys all the time. "Tell me about yourself, Travis Bennett. You look like you're doing pretty well in Tinsel Town."

Travis nodded quickly. "Oh. Sure. I even have a recording deal."

"Really?"

Travis cleared his throat. "Uh. Yeah. I'm cutting my first album. That's why I'm afraid I won't be able to drive you to your audition tomorrow. I'll be in the studio all morning."

"Oh!" Liza shook her head. "I wouldn't dream of asking you. You're so busy and everything . . ."

"Why don't I pick you up after?" Travis offered. "Around four o'clock? I'll show you around town."

"Thank you," Liza said calmly. Inside she was doing cartwheels, barely able to believe her good fortune.

"You can tell me all about Winnie and how she's doing," Travis added.

"Okay," Liza said absently, staring at a block-long limousine passing them on the freeway. "Winnie," she repeated. "Oh, yes. Winnie . . ."

Travis nodded, smiling. "It was sure great to hear her voice on my phone machine yesterday when she asked me to pick you up. I haven't seen her since I dropped in on her at the U. of S. last fall."

Liza spotted a freeway sign that said Hollywood. "I can't believe I'm really here. Hollywood. *Hollywood.* How could such an exciting name be on something dull like a freeway exit sign? Hollywood isn't a city. It's a dream. It's the end of the rainbow."

"We had some great times together in Europe," Travis continued. "She was my first love."

"Look!" Liza squealed as she caught sight of the giant letters in the scrubby hills that spelled H-O-L-L-Y-W-O-O-D. She was barely paying attention to Travis now, but tried to act as if she were interested in his reminiscences about Winnie. "I hardly see Winnie anymore," Liza muttered, her eyes dazzled by the sleek BMWs and Jaguars zooming by.

"Why's that?" Travis asked casually, flicking on his turn signal.

"Well, ever since she married Josh, she's been living off campus," Liza noted.

*SCREEEEEEECH!* The car tires screamed.

Liza cried out as the sedan veered to the right, nearly colliding with the astonished man in the car only inches away from Liza. Quickly, the driver pulled away from Travis's drifting car, shaking his fist. *"LOOK OUT!"*

Travis jerked the car back into his lane and it nearly smashed into the guardrail.

For a second, Liza thought Travis was going to total the car. Everything was moving very fast and horns honked from all directions. She looked over at Travis and saw that his face had turned pale and his mouth had dropped open. "Travis!"

Travis quickly straightened the car and stared stonily ahead. "Sorry."

Liza gasped and clutched her chest, breathing hard as the car swooped beneath a series of overpasses. "You scared me to death!"

"Sorry about that," Travis said quietly. "I . . . uh . . . something flew into my eye."

Liza sighed and looked ahead. There was a moment of silence before Travis finally spoke up.

"So, uh, Winnie is married?" he asked quietly.

Liza shrugged. "Yeah. She married a guy named Josh Gaffey a few weeks ago. They seem really happy."

"But I—" Travis began, then shut his mouth tightly. The car drove onto Sunset Boulevard and Liza stared wide-eyed at the gritty scenes below the high-flying palm trees. It was Hollywood, but there were also a lot of everyday things going on. They passed supermarkets, dry cleaners, record stores, Mexican restaurants. There were poor people on the sidewalks and rich people in cars. And everywhere, noise and smog and reminders that it wasn't really the end of the rainbow. It was somewhere in the middle.

Liza looked over at Travis as he pulled up to the Tropicana Motel, realizing that they hadn't talked since the freeway. "Thanks, Travis. I really appreciate it. Are we still on for four o'clock tomorrow?"

"Sure," Travis said shortly, getting out and handing Liza's large suitcase to her. "Good luck."

"Thanks," Liza said as Travis quickly got back into the car and sped away. "It was nice meeting you," she whispered. "Really nice."

# Three

Lauren's red marker pen made squeaky sounds as she read through Dash Ramirez's half of their popular "His/Her" column for the *U. of S. Weekly Journal.*

"*Embarrassment* has two *r*s and two *s*s," Lauren muttered to herself, irritably slashing an upside down "v" in the middle of the word and adding an extra letter. "*Accommodate* has two *c*s and two *m*s."

Lauren gritted her teeth and stared absently at her roommate, Melissa McDormand, who was pumping five-pound weights on the other side of her dorm room, making annoying little puffing noises as she exhaled.

Listening to Melissa was almost as nerve-racking as

thinking about her ex-boyfriend and column-partner, Dash. Lately, he'd been hanging around, trying to get back together with her.

Dash Ramirez. First he talks me into falling in love with him. Then he boosts my confidence, she thought. Then he dumps me when I get too assertive for him. Then, just when he's about to convince me to get back together with him, he takes off with sorority princess Courtney Conner.

Now Lauren was convinced that the only one she could really count on was herself. Everyone else was unreliable. Everyone else was irritating her to death.

Dash. Melissa. Everyone!

All she could do now was focus on her writing and her self-defense class. Mental and physical toughness would see her through.

Lauren wondered why she'd ever been stupid enough to move out of Faith's dorm room. Faith was the *only* person she'd ever been able to count on. In fact, Lauren thought sadly, if Faith were sitting in front of her right now, instead of Melissa, she would have a lot of things sorted out.

Faith was the only person who understood, even when Lauren had been a scared, overprotected, newly arrived freshman trying to throw off the chains of her wealthy parents.

All Melissa could do was pump iron and complain about her personal life.

Faith helped her find the courage to submit her first piece to the *Journal*.

All Melissa did was distract her from her work and drag her down into her miserable depressions.

Lauren gripped her pen and continued slashing at the page. She shook her wispy brown hair and glanced down at the printout. The "His/Her" column was the student newspaper's hottest feature. So hot, in fact, that she and Dash had to keep churning it out, even though they were barely speaking.

*Sure, it would be great to get back with Dash and make it work the way it used to,* Lauren thought miserably. *But what if we break up again? Why should I put myself through the same agony twice? How can I ever trust a man again? Maybe Faith would have the answer, but I don't. There's just no way. I'm getting my life back together, but alone.*

"What's—your—column—on—this—week?" Melissa gasped as she strained her forearm up. She sat back and slipped on her Walkman headset. Her short red hair hung limply around her face and she was breathing hard.

Lauren rolled her eyes. "It's about sexual harassment on campus. We're using the Courtney Conner case. You know, the sorority president who accused the economist she was interning with?"

Melissa nodded and wiped her face with a towel. "Yeah. Eric Sutter. She said he threatened to flunk her if she didn't sleep with him."

"According to Courtney, anyway. But who knows what really happened." Lauren bent her head back down to her work, desperately wishing Melissa would leave for the library. All she wanted was a few moments of peace. If she heard Melissa grunt one more time, she'd be tempted to throw her word processor across the room at her.

Melissa grabbed the dumbbell again and began working her other arm. "I think she was telling the truth."

Lauren scribbled something in the margin. "Uh-huh. That's what everyone says," she answered, her voice dripping with sarcasm. "That's what Dash says. And he should know. He's a really close friend of hers."

"Whoa," Melissa grunted. "I can't tell whose side you're on or anything."

Lauren glared at her for a moment, then looked down. Of course Melissa would say that. Everyone believed beautiful, smart, thin, in-control Courtney. And Dash. Well, Dash had fallen all over himself trying to help Courtney uncover Sutter's history of harassing women on university campuses.

That would have been fine with Lauren if Courtney had meant nothing to Dash. But Dash had been involved with the snobby sorority president and it was clear that she still meant a lot to him. The proof was in the fact that even after Dash had promised Lauren he'd forget Courtney, the first thing he did was go off and rescue her from Eric Sutter.

"Are you actually defending Eric Sutter in your half of the column?" Melissa asked. By this time, she had switched to a ten-pound weight. Lauren could see the veins in Melissa's neck sticking out a little. Her well-developed biceps were sweaty.

Lauren heaved a huge sigh, continuing to look down impatiently at Dash's copy. Faith would understand. "I'm *not* defending harassers, if that's what you mean. I'm discussing how these harassment complaints can actually end up hurting women in the workplace, because men are afraid to hire them."

"Oh, right," Melissa cracked.

Lauren looked at Melissa coldly. "Believe me, it would be easier to make the opposite argument. If you want to know the truth, I don't trust men at all anymore. But Dash Ramirez has the privilege of being politically correct this week, not me."

There was a long silence as Melissa glared back at Lauren, then looked down, continuing to pump. Actually, Lauren felt a tiny bit guilty for snapping at Melissa like that. Only a few weeks before, Melissa had been deserted at the altar by her fiancé, Brooks Baldwin, Faith's old boyfriend. Right after that Lauren had become Melissa's roommate in Forest Hall. But even though Lauren had spent a lot of time trying to be supportive to Melissa, the whole experience had only made Lauren miserable, too.

Lauren had decided then to end her midnight pig

outs and all-night complaining sessions with Melissa. Ever since, Melissa had been bitter about the change.

"Ugh," Melissa groaned. Lauren looked down and saw that her roommate had slipped down to the floor and had begun a series of push-ups. It was strange, but Melissa had mysteriously snapped out of her funk right when Lauren decided to pull back.

As Lauren watched Melissa's well-toned body bob up and down on the floor, she thought her roommate looked anything but down. In fact, she'd never seen Melissa so strong and determined. Lauren had worried that Melissa wouldn't hold on to her track scholarship, but no more. And if Melissa started hitting the books, Lauren was sure Melissa could salvage her perfect premed GPA.

"Why are you staring at me?" Melissa burst out, sitting up and looking hard at Lauren with eyes that looked like two red-hot coals.

Lauren's mouth dropped open. "I . . . uh . . . was just thinking. I mean, you're so together, Melissa."

"Right," Melissa sneered.

"What?"

"You don't sound very sincere," Melissa snapped.

Lauren looked at her. "I don't get it. One minute you're chatting and working out. The next minute you're getting worked up over nothing."

Melissa stood up and gave Lauren a menacing look. Then she put a towel around her neck. "This is not nothing. This is how I feel, Lauren. Do you understand?"

"Melissa . . ." Lauren began, shocked. Sure, she hadn't been spending as much time with Melissa. Yes, she was irritable and preoccupied tonight with the stupid column. But why was Melissa exploding like this?

"Oh, don't even try," Melissa drawled. "I'm sick of your coldness and your snobbery. You're so phony. You pretend to be a feminist and a journalist, but you're still just a spoiled little rich girl."

Lauren's hand went up to her mouth in shock.

"You think things are so tough," Melissa continued, stretching out her leg muscles. "You don't know what tough is. Look at you with your brand-new Jeep and your fancy boarding school manners. I hate to break it to you, Lauren, but you look really silly in your expensive combat pants and your phony self-defense postures."

Lauren could barely speak. "What's wrong, Mel?" she whispered. "I'm sorry I snapped at you, but . . ."

Melissa threw back her head and laughed. "Oh, God, it feels great. So great. At last I have the guts to tell people what I really think. Now if I could only run into Brooks, I'd tell him what I really think about him, too."

Lowering her eyes back down to the column, Lauren didn't know what to say or think. Shy, hard-working Melissa had gone through so many personality changes in the last few months, Lauren barely knew who the real Melissa was anymore. But as Melissa finished her workout with her stretching exercises, Lauren was sure of one thing.

If it was the only thing she did this week, she would catch up with Faith. She absolutely had to talk to her. About Dash. About Melissa. About taking risks. About everything that seemed to be getting crazier each day.

Only Faith could help her sort out her life.

# *Four*

F aith opened her eyes, closed them again, and buried herself deeper under her flannel blanket.

It was Tuesday morning. Faith had three days left to think of the most brilliant, original *Taming of the Shrew* ever produced on the American stage. Two days left to memorize two hundred and fifty years of European history in time for Professor Hermann's Western Civ exam.

The entire situation was getting out of hand. It was hopeless. Faith turned dejectedly over, thinking how the university could possibly expect students to be creative when they piled on the coursework and stuffed everyone into dorms where no one had a moment of peace and quiet.

Faith sighed. The night before she'd even dragged herself across campus to the library, hoping that a change of locale would charge her imagination.

She wanted to be in the Theater Program more than she wanted anything in her life, but her brain wasn't working. And sitting in the library had been about as stimulating as a date with a file cabinet.

A wave of fresh air suddenly rippled over Faith's face. She looked groggily out at the room and wondered where Liza's mountains of clothes, costume jewelry, and junk food containers had gone.

Then something clicked.

Liza was in L.A. The person she'd shared the room with all night wasn't noisy, disorganized, boisterous Liza Ruff.

Her roommate at that moment was Becker Cain.

Mr. Neat. Mr. Considerate. Becker Cain. He had been asleep by the time she'd stumbled in from the library the night before. She blinked when she finally focused on his empty bed.

Propping herself up on her elbow to get a better look, Faith's eyes got wider at the sight. His narrow bed had been made neatly. His books were stacked on his desk. And Liza's junk had been neatly stowed away. The only sign of his presence was a copy of Nietzsche's *Beyond Good and Evil* lying open on his pillow.

Then she looked over at her desk and drew in her breath sharply. Fluttering in front of her open window was one yellow wildflower in a tin can. On a plate next to it was a simple arrangement of fruit and bread from the dining commons. Next to that was a thermos. She crawled out of bed, lifted the lid of the thermos, and was greeted with the inviting aroma of steaming hot coffee.

Becker had done this. She took a bite of the fresh bread and chewed it thoughtfully. Why?

Faith lay back, took another bite, and nestled her hand under her head. Someone had actually done something for her. It seemed strange. She couldn't remember when it happened last. She enjoyed organizing people and taking charge. But the more she thought about it, the more it seemed like that was *all* she'd been doing since she'd arrived on campus last September.

*Maybe that's one of the reasons I'm going crazy,* she thought.

Faith took a few moments to savor the peace and quiet. Becker had only been there one night, but her everyday life already seemed completely different. The dresser that usually overflowed with Liza's scarves, scripts, jewelry, and stockings was suddenly bare. Now it held a single cup with a toothbrush standing in it, a brush, and a plate with a few coins in it. The faint scent of after-shave lingered in the air and a man's T-shirt hung over the back of Liza's desk chair.

Faith sipped some coffee, stood up, and padded across the room in her oversized T-shirt. It was the first coed morning in the hall. She wanted to make sure the coast was clear before she ducked into the bathroom.

Faith peeked through a crack in the door and saw a well-built guy emerging from what was once the girls' bathroom, wearing only a white towel wrapped around his waist.

Faith's eyes hung on his muscular physique for a moment before her eyes traveled up to his face and she suddenly recognized him.

It was Becker.

"Becker?" Faith whispered, trying to suppress a gasp. It seemed impossible that this was the same bookish guy in the dark clothes and baggy jacket she'd met the afternoon before. His smooth, muscled torso was connected to a pair of wide shoulders that looked as if they were meant to lift heavy equipment, not slim volumes of philosophical essays.

"Hi," he said lightly as Faith silently opened the door for him. He gave her a puzzled smile as he passed her in the doorway. Faith realized it must have seemed she was waiting for him. "How did you sleep?"

"Uh, fine," Faith managed, turning and flattening

up against the door as he passed, unable to take her eyes off him. Becker's wet dark hair was neatly slicked back. Yesterday, it had covered half his face. This morning, she could see the strong bones in his face and his high, smooth brow. Becker Cain wasn't just a good-looking guy. He was gorgeous.

Suddenly Faith realized that Becker, who had begun to put his shampoo away, had half turned to stare back at her. With a smaller towel, he began briskly rubbing his hair dry. "Faith?" Becker said evenly. "Would you mind turning away for a few minutes while I get dressed?"

Faith tore her eyes away from the drops of water rolling down his muscled back. She felt her face turn red. In her shock at seeing Becker half-naked, she'd forgotten that she was barely covered herself. Quickly, she grabbed her bathrobe from the hook on the back of the door and covered her sleepshirt. "A-actually, it's my turn to head for the shower now, I guess," she stammered.

Becker crossed his arms in front of his bare chest and leaned against the dresser. "I would have warned you I was going to use the bathroom, Faith," he explained. "But I didn't want to wake you."

Faith tied her bathrobe at the waist nervously. "Oh. Uh, no. I mean, that's okay."

For a moment Becker and Faith looked at each other, each not knowing what to say. Then Faith turned and grabbed her flowered cosmetic bag from the top of her dresser. "I'll be back in a few." She backed up to open a drawer and pulled out a shirt and a pair of jeans. When she did she felt Becker bump against her.

"Oops," Becker said softly.

"Oh," Faith whispered. "Sorry."

Faith hurried to the bathroom, found that it was empty, and quickly showered. When she got out, a girl from down the hall was irritably brushing her teeth at the sink.

"Hi, Sandy," Faith said, unzipping her cosmetic bag and pulling out a comb and a bottle of lotion. "Aren't you in the Coed-by-Bed experiment, too?"

Sandy spat her toothpaste out and took a sip of water. "Oh, yeah," she said sarcastically. "Brilliant idea on my part. The guy's a complete jerk. Made dumb jokes all afternoon. Invited his Neanderthal jock buddies over for the evening. And snored all night. If I can't get rid of him by afternoon, I'm moving out for the week."

"Gee," Faith said softly, running a comb through her hair. "That's terrible. I thought they screened out guys like that from the program."

"Come on," Sandy said bitterly. "How can you possibly know what a guy's *really* like until you have to live with him?"

"You're right," Faith said in a whisper. "I guess I lucked out this time."

A few minutes later, she'd dressed and finished combing out her long wet hair. She added a little blusher as an afterthought, and hurried back down the hall, her spirits lifting with each step. Maybe Becker Cain was just the person she needed right now to jolt her out of her miserable creative slump. At the very least, he was a huge improvement over Liza.

Becker was sitting cross-legged on his bed, sipping coffee from a mug, and reading Nietzsche when she opened the door. Wearing an open-necked white shirt, black pants, and a pair of small, round reading glasses, he was the picture of calm and concentration.

*Here is someone who actually has his act together,* Faith thought, glancing briefly over at him as she put her stuff away. *An endangered species on this campus.*

"Thanks for the coffee and breakfast, by the way," Faith said shyly, slipping her underwear into her closet. She'd never realized how small her room was. Becker would never be more than four feet away from her all week.

Becker smiled and stretched his long legs. He took off his glasses and rubbed his eyes with one hand. "When you didn't come down to the dining commons for breakfast, I decided you'd slept in. I thought you'd like something to eat."

"I am starved," Faith admitted, trying to remember the last time anyone had stopped to think of what *she* might like.

Becker held up his coffee mug. "I took the liberty of sharing some of the coffee with you." He shook his head, and his brow furrowed in mock seriousness. "Caffeine. My only vice."

Faith let out a gentle laugh as she poured more into her own mug. "You call coffee a vice? Come on. I can think of a lot of other vices going on around us, like drugs and alcohol. Compared to everyone else, that's nothing."

Becker grabbed his pillow and stuffed it behind his back. His handsome face looked thoughtful, though his eyes were crinkled and twinkling at her. "Yes, but we're not everyone."

"Oh, right," Faith murmured. The way he said it made them sound like a couple. Her eyes shyly darted across the room, then fell back down into her coffee cup.

Becker took a long, thoughtful sip of coffee, set it down, and looked up at the ceiling. There was an intensity in his pale, clear eyes. "Why compare yourself to people whose values you don't respect? They shouldn't enter into the picture when you are deciding how to live your life."

Faith stared at him, mesmerized, as she bit into another piece of bread. "I never really looked at it that way."

"But Faith," Becker replied, closing his book and setting it down. "You are an artist."

"Well, I . . ."

"The fact sheet they gave me said you were a theater arts major," Becker continued.

"Yes, I am."

"So . . ." Becker went on. "Then you spend a lot of time observing and interpreting life as you see it. Right?" He propped himself up on his elbow and gazed at her. "You have to be independent and creative. You can't get bogged down comparing yourself to ordinary people and their ordinary problems."

Faith's brain was whirring. In a way, she agreed with Becker. Sometimes it *was* hard to spend so much time with other people when she knew she should be spending more time thinking and reading. But wasn't Becker taking the idea a little too far?

"I partly agree," Faith replied, stretching out her own legs, suddenly grateful that she'd actually had a clean pair of jeans to wear that morning. "But I also believe that artists have to understand—and empathize with the problems others are having."

"But do you have to be a part of it to see it?" Becker's eyes were twinkling at her. The shape of his face and the paleness of his skin made him look aristocratic, almost princely. She found herself mentally dressing him in an Elizabethan costume. Tights. Velvet cloak. A golden crown . . .

"Uh-huh," Faith mumbled.

"No, really," Becker insisted, staring at her.

Faith blinked. "Um. Well, I'm not sure. I've been involved with everyone's problems for so long, I don't know what it would be like to be separated from them. But it isn't giving me much time to nurture my creative side this week."

"Your friends," Becker said with a knowing look, and Faith found herself smiling at him. "Oh!" Becker reached out a long arm and handed her a slip of paper. "This message for you was taped to our door this morning."

Faith looked at it.

The note was from Lauren.

WE HAVE TO TALK NOW!!! Faith read. Lauren had signed it L.T.S.

"Boyfriend?" Becker asked with a curious lift to one eyebrow.

"Oh, no," Faith answered wearily, twisting a strand of her hair with her finger. She felt like balling up the note and throwing it in the wastebasket. Dealing with Lauren these days was like putting in a full day as a lion tamer in a traveling circus. Faith felt as if she needed to pick up a chair just to defend herself against Lauren's anger.

Lauren's anti-male ravings.

Lauren's emotional pleas for heart-to-heart talks and midnight coffees.

For once, Faith absolutely didn't have time to talk!

"Your brother," Becker deadpanned.

"No." Faith sighed and smiled at the same time. "Just a friend. Lauren Turnbell-Smythe. She used to be my shy, quiet roommate. Now she's one of the top writers on the *Journal* and one of the most intensely political friends I've ever had. She's going through a hard time right now."

Becker frowned. "You're always surrounded by people, Faith. I sometimes see you in the dining commons. Not once have I seen you alone."

Faith shrugged and breathed in deeply. She took another sip of coffee and glanced across the room. Becker was staring at her with a mixture of sympathy and admiration. There was something relaxed and unthreatening about Becker that she was beginning to like. "I am close to a lot of people. It's always been that way for me."

"But are you really close?" Becker asked, his brow furrowing with sincere concern. Faith pictured him as a dashing theater director. A stunt pilot. A world traveler returning home to write about his mystical experiences in the Himalayas. He was probably the most exotic-looking, handsome guy she'd ever seen. "I mean, how close can you get to any one person when your time is spread out between so many?"

Faith grinned. "Whew," she joked, "you aren't a philosophy major or anything, are you?"

Becker's face was serious. He stood up and walked toward the window, slipping his glasses back on. "Don't mind me. It's just that my father always says that. He talks a lot about time and about how people waste it. Then they end up wasting their whole lives," he said softly. "Maybe I'm just mimicking him."

Faith opened her mouth and dropped a grape in. Suddenly the room had become very silent. "He did?" she whispered, trying to think why she was lowering her voice. She was beginning to wonder how the conversation had become so personal—so fast.

"He and my mother are musicians," Becker said, his jaw muscles tightening a little. "She's a violinist. He plays the viola. They're part of a touring classical group that's done very well. The Metropolitan String Quartet. Maybe you've heard of them."

Faith's eyebrows shot up. She'd heard them play at a music festival near Jacksonville. The performance had been electrifying. And she'd remembered the musicians. Intense. Full of energy and dedication. The one woman, who must have been Becker's mother, had the same long, dark hair and porcelain skin. "Yes." Faith breathed. "I've seen them in concert."

Becker nodded as if it were nothing unusual. "They've traveled all over the world. Together, they've developed an amazing repertoire. Music surrounded me when I was a child. But they were gone almost the entire time I was growing up, though I had a nanny to take care of me and a big New York apartment to play in. Now I understand. They had each other."

"It must have been lonely for you," Faith said, sipping her coffee, starting to feel self-conscious again. "But if I'd known you in high school, I would have been a little jealous. My dad ran his veterinary practice right out of our house. My parents were right on top of me every second."

"That could be good, too," Becker said simply, staring off with a lost look on his face.

Faith looked down. Becker was nice, but the minutes were ticking away. "I've got to study, Becker." She tried to sound energetic. "Like your dad would say: time's a wastin'."

"Yeah, yeah," Becker turned toward her. "You told me all about it just before you left for the library last night. Thursday: big test. Friday: big presentation. What's the problem? You've got plenty of time."

"Are you kidding?" Faith rolled her eyes, yanking her theater notebook off her desk. "The exam is halfway under control, but the presentation on *Shrew* is nowhere. I've got to come up with something fresh and original in the next few days or I can kiss the professional theater program good-bye."

"You don't have a time problem, Faith," Becker insisted. "You have a concentration problem."

"Yeah, that too." Faith sighed.

"What you need," Becker began, sitting up, "is someone to help you focus your mind. In order to be creative you have to be focused. And you have to be relaxed. Come on. Let's go up to the dorm roof. You can review your ideas out loud and I'll listen."

Faith was surprised to feel relief at Becker's offer. Something made her want to believe him. Or maybe she figured he was her last chance. In any case, within a few minutes she was following Becker obediently up the stairs to the roof, where he spread out a gray blanket and sat cross-legged on it. His long hair, now dry, was blowing in the morning breeze, and he had a serene look on his face.

Faith breathed in the cool air and watched a group of sparrows hop across the tar and gravel surface. "What about you, Becker?" she suddenly wanted to know. "If your method works and you help me, how will I pay you back? Will you let me help you study?"

Throwing his head back, Becker gave a small laugh. "Philosophy exams are so weird. It's hard to describe how I study for them. It's more a matter of thinking through the connections, so that I can answer the extremely odd essay questions my professors give me." He shook his head. "Don't worry about me. I'm ahead in my classes and I've got time to spare."

"Well," Faith flopped herself down on the edge of the blanket. "*The Taming of the Shrew* is a tricky play," she began. "The main character . . ."

"Katharina . . ." Becker urged her on, nodding.

"Yeah."

"Angry," Becker noted.

"But not crazy angry. She knows what she wants."

"In the end, she pretends to be Petruchio's slave."

"But she's not," Faith nodded eagerly. "She's his equal."

"She's winking at the world."

"Yeah."

Becker was nodding, too. "So you need a wild spirit to the play."

"A sense of fun. A sense of being two people at once . . ." Faith was starting to giggle.

"She's a witch!"

"She's a circus clown!"

Faith was suddenly digging for ideas, her mind recharged. Before she knew it, she was telling Becker a thousand things about her hopes and dreams of a career in the theater. Things she'd never told anyone, not even her best friends.

Faith looked over at Becker lying on his back, staring up at the sky. Maybe he was right. Time wasn't her enemy. *She* was her own worst enemy if she let everything else in her life sap her energy and throw it out of focus.

And maybe she'd found someone who really understood.

# Five

························

*C*lick, click, click. Nnnnnuhhhhhh. Tap. Tap. Eeeeeuuuuh.

Winnie looked up from her nest of Western Civ study notes and stared at Josh's back. The blue light from his computer seemed like a beacon in the fading bedroom light. It made her feel lonely, as if he were a thousand miles away instead of at the other end of their bedroom.

Since their spontaneous wedding a few weeks ago, Winnie and Josh had been living off-campus in a charming bungalow found by one of their roommates, Clifford Bronton. Out of the dorms and together at last, Winnie and Josh were probably the happiest cou-

ple west of the Mississippi. They had been ready to
make a commitment. Marriage was the best thing that
had ever happened to either one of them.

Until they found out last week that Winnie was
pregnant.

Sitting cross-legged on her rumpled bed, she
looked back down at her sea of books, notebooks,
sheets of paper and little yellow Post-It notes scattered everywhere on the ink-stained bedspread. But
she didn't want to study the Italian Renaissance anymore. She knew it by heart.

She wanted to talk to Josh.

And she desperately needed a heart-to-heart with
Faith. *Nnnnnnnhhhh. Click, click, click.* Josh continued tapping at the keyboard, pausing, thinking, sighing, and staring up at the ceiling as if his computer
were the most important thing in the world.

"Josh?"

*Tap. Tap. Tap. Tap.* Pause.

Winnie crossed her arms angrily. Josh wasn't going
to talk to her. And she was having a terrible time getting a hold of Faith.

*Faith Crowley. My best friend and she doesn't even know
I'm pregnant,* Winnie thought. *She never has time any
more. She doesn't return my phone calls. I need to see her
alone—desperately. She's the only one who'd really understand. She's the only one who can help me figure out how to
handle this!*

"Josh?"

*Click. Click. Click.*

Winnie shoved her notebooks aside and stretched her legs out, growing more impatient by the second. Her 1950s green silk bathrobe had creases in it from sitting in one place for so long. She stared down at her stomach. Her still-flat stomach. Why wouldn't he talk to her?

*Tap. Tap.*

*"JOSH!"* she nearly screeched.

"Uh-huh?" Josh came back. He turned briefly to look at Winnie and gave her a guilty smile. His dark hair flopped over his deep-set eyes and his bare feet were hooked around the legs of his chair. "Just a sec, Win. Just let me reformat this hard disk and I'm done."

"You said that half an hour ago," Winnie snapped.

"Win."

Winnie flopped back onto her pillow and stared at the ceiling, trying to remember the last time she tried to leave a message with Faith. Wasn't it only last night? Why hadn't she called back?

Faith always called her back. She was so reliable. Winnie calls. Faith calls back. They talk. Winnie feels better. Why was Faith suddenly avoiding her at the very moment she needed her most?

"This is starting to remind me of a 'Star Trek' I saw once where the Starship *Enterprise* was stuck in some kind of time-space continuum," Winnie began loudly.

*Tap. Tap. Tap. Tap.*

"Anyway," Winnie continued, trying not to notice that Josh was ignoring her, "everybody on the ship starts to feel like they've said and done everything a dozen times before."

*Click. Nnnnnuuuuhhh.*

"It turned out it was because the spaceship was stuck in some sort of time warp," Winnie went on, tears now spilling out of her eyes and down her cheeks, "and it wasn't until everyone started getting really bad déjà-vu and tripping out on it that they stopped themselves and managed to get out of the time warp."

"Oh, no," Josh mumbled, still staring at the computer screen.

"Oh, yes." Winnie nodded, yanking a tissue and blowing her nose. "And that's what's happening to us, Josh. Married only a few weeks and we're stuck in a time warp. Saying the same things over and over and over again."

"Unbelievable."

"I know," Winnie answered. "I mean, listen to us. I keep saying, 'Josh, we have to talk.' You keep saying, 'Just a minute, Win.' I keep saying, 'But Josh, I'm pregnant now and we have to plan for this baby.' And you keep saying, 'Okay, Win, as soon as I finish reformatting this—'" Winnie broke off as a tired, sick feeling swept over her. She laid her head down on the pillow.

"This is terrible," Josh murmured.

"I know it, Josh," Winnie groaned. "But we just have to get through it."

"You have to look at this, Win," Josh whispered, finally looking away from the screen. Wearing his usual bleach-stained T-shirt and ragged, army-green sweatpants, Josh's face looked weary and drawn. In one ear he wore a tiny blue earring. His eyes narrowed with concern when he saw her. "What's wrong?"

Winnie sobbed. "You haven't been listening to a word I said."

"But Win," Josh said urgently, tapping a key. "I just found a file in the system I thought I'd erased. It's that letterhead I helped Rich with."

Winnie plumped her pillow with her fist and slammed the side of her face down on it. "Really?"

Rich Greenberg was one of their housemates. Last week, Josh had helped him design a fancy congratulation announcement on the computer for his girlfriend, Liza Ruff. The relationship had always seemed a little odd to Josh and Winnie. After all, Liza had been the one who'd stolen his ventriloquist's dummy and had ruined his chances to win the campus comedy contest. But Rich still seemed to be crazy about her.

Josh shook his head in disbelief. "The document was supposed to be a sort of congratulatory letter after Liza won that spot on the cable TV show featuring the best campus comedy acts."

"Yeah." Winnie sighed.

"But he changed it."

"Josh. We have to talk.'

Josh scratched his forehead. "Now it's a letterhead, from Bernie Greenberg Productions, Inc. His dad's firm in L.A. It looks like *Rich* was the one who wrote that letter to Liza, inviting her to Hollywood for the screen test. Not his big-shot dad. Rich faked the letterhead."

For a moment Winnie forgot her own troubles. She lifted her head up from the pillow. "He set her up," Winnie said slowly. "He *was* mad when he found out Liza had sabotaged his own chances to win the campus comedy contest."

"Yeah."

"And now she's spent all her money so that she can get totally humiliated in L.A.," Winnie said sadly.

"We've got to warn her." Josh was cradling his forehead in his hand. "Call your friend Travis or something. I never would have guessed it. Rich doesn't seem like the nasty type."

"No, at least he didn't," Winnie replied, noticing the topic of the conversation had changed again. Was Josh actually trying to get her to drop the whole subject of her pregnancy?

"So, will you call her?" Josh said. "It's important."

Winnie faced Josh with wet eyes. "What's *really* important right now, Josh Gaffey, is that I am *preg-*

*nant* and we have to talk. This is not something that's going to go away."

Josh shoved his keyboard forward and buried his face in his hands. Winnie could see his back muscles tensing under his T-shirt. "I know, I know," he mumbled. He sat up and swiveled his chair around. Then he gave her a look of sheer misery that made Winnie's heart break. She had never seen his dark eyes look so defeated. So scared. "What do you want me to say?"

Winnie felt her will crumple. If only she'd been able to talk to Faith first. Faith could have helped her prepare for Josh's weird behavior. Letting out a deep sob, Winnie lay her head back on the pillow. "I don't know!" she cried. "How about: 'Everything's going to be okay, Win.' Or: 'We're in this together, Win.' Hey, here's another good one: 'I'll love you forever no matter what happens.'"

Josh looked stunned. "That's all you need? That's going to make it all better for you?"

"It would be a *start*," Winnie cried out.

Josh stood up and began pacing the room slowly. "The fact is, Winnie, things are *not* okay."

"Well, we're just going to have to adjust somehow," Winnie barked back.

Josh stopped suddenly in the middle of the room. He had a wild, helpless look in his eyes. "How . . . did . . . this . . . happen?" he asked slowly, as if the terrible realization had finally sunk in. "Things like this don't happen to people like us. We're supposed to be the smart ones. The ones who know all about birth control. The ones who go to college and do productive things. . . ."

"You know exactly what happened," Winnie practically screamed. "We went for a picnic in the mountains."

Josh rubbed his forehead and began backing away from her. "Right. You insisted. It was a beautiful day. Right, Winnie? Then you forgot to bring the birth control."

Tear's ran down Winnie's face. "We *both* forgot the birth control. But you wanted to . . ."

"You said you thought it would be okay," Josh roared. "You said you were pretty sure you couldn't get pregnant at that time of the month."

"I did not," Winnie yelled back. "I said I didn't think so, but that I wasn't sure. Then, *you* got carried away!"

"Oh! So it's *my* fault!" Josh cried, swinging himself around, nearly knocking over the lamp on the dresser.

"The point is," Winnie tried to lower her voice and gather her wits. "The point is that we have to figure out how we're going to take care of the baby."

"The baby," Josh echoed. "The baby."

"Yes, the baby," Winnie cried out, grabbing a stack of study notes and throwing them at Josh. The air was suddenly filled with papers fluttering crazily to the bedroom floor. "Someone has to take care of the baby! And if it's going to be me, I might as well drop out now so I can get a job and save up some money."

"Oh, Winnie," Josh broke down, sobbing and collapsing on the bed, then into her arms.

"What's the point of studying the Italian Renaissance," Winnie's voice was cracking, "when I have to start thinking about caring for a baby?" Overcome with tears, she buried her wet face in Josh's neck.

"You can't drop out," Josh said softly, wrapping his arms around her tightly. "We've both got to stay in school somehow."

"But how?"

"I don't know, Win," Josh wept. "I just don't know yet."

Brooks Baldwin swung his sturdy leg over the seat of the leg press in the steamy U. of S. weight room. He quietly took in the familiar sound of straining bodies and creaking weight machine chains. Then he glanced over at the tall stack of black, twenty-pound weights.

"One hundred for starters," Brooks muttered to himself, slipping the metal pin in place. He lay back and positioned his feet on the metal plates. Then he took a deep breath and pushed his feet forward mightily. It felt good to be back. He'd pumped a little iron last fall during soccer season. Then again earlier in the spring, just so he could be with Melissa when she worked out.

Melissa.

Brooks's sense of well-being suddenly dissolved into guilt. Heavy, paralyzing, all-consuming guilt. Guilt so thick and heavy he was swimming in it. Drowning in it. Every day.

Melissa.

The girl he thought he loved. The girl he'd proposed to and practically pledged his life to, until he left her standing at the altar only a few weeks before.

And now had to deal with it. Somehow.

Brooks pushed off again smoothly, feeling the steady burn in his thighs and calves. Already sweat was breaking out on his forehead and back. He'd been away too long.

"Three," Brooks moaned, gradually pulling his legs up again. His knee cartilage creaked. It was going to take a while to get back into top form. He'd been avoiding the gym since he broke up with Melissa, mostly because he'd been afraid of bumping into her. He was avoiding everything that reminded him of her. The workouts. Her friends. Even the library.

"Four," he grunted. At least he'd studied a lot. Constant reading and thinking were the only things that kept his guilt at bay. Working out left his mind too free to think about how he'd messed up her life, just so he could save his own from a terrible mistake.

"Faith," Brooks whispered to himself. "If only I could talk to Faith about this. We were together for so many years. She was the only one who really understood me. Who took the time to listen. I could always sort out my thoughts with her."

Brooks pushed out again and ignored the searing pain. The blood was pumping into his head and his eyes felt as if they were about to pop out.

"Want me to take that weight down for you a little?" Brooks heard a familiar voice behind him. He lowered the weight carefully and looked around.

It was Melissa. Something twisted inside him.

"Hi," Brooks panted. He sat up and stared at her. Her freckled arms and legs were glistening with sweat, her face was flushed, and her eyes had an unyielding gleam in them that he didn't recognize.

"What brings you here?" Melissa drawled, clutching the ends of the short, white gym towel around her neck. She casually lifted one of her strong legs and rested it against the side of Brooks's leg press.

Brooks couldn't help staring at her. She looked as beautiful and strong as she did when they were together. Her eyes were sparkling, her cheeks were flushed, and she was in perfect shape. Brooks thought back to the way she looked a week or so after their canceled wedding. She'd been pale and bleary-eyed. But now it looked as if Melissa had been working out practically every hour since he left her at the altar. He cleared his throat. "Just trying to get back into it." Brooks managed a guilty smile. "But I feel like a ninety-pound weakling."

"Nah," Melissa scoffed. "Suck it in. You can do it."

Brooks stared at her hard face, then realized he couldn't think of anything else to say. "Come on, Mel," he heard himself say, just to break the silence. "Challenge."

"All right!" Melissa chuckled, whipping off her towel and settling easily onto the leg press next to his. She leaned over. "Come on. What are you pressing?" Her eyebrows shot up with amazement. "One hundred? Hey, you *are* a ninety-pound weakling. Let's get it up to one-fifty or you're gonna get sand kicked in your face this summer, big guy."

Brooks frowned. This didn't sound like the quiet, determined Melissa he almost married. Seeing her now made him even more sure that he'd done the right thing. There always had been something about Melissa he didn't quite understand. Something hard and desperate lurking just under the surface that he could never reach. "Okay, Mel," he agreed, slipping the extra weights in place and bracing his feet.

"Go!" Melissa said, a defiant edge in her voice, easily pressing the weight forward and drawing it back with her powerful muscles.

Brooks shoved the metal plates forward with all his

might, barely getting a full extension of his legs. Exhausted, he slammed the weights back in place.

"Uh-oh," Melissa warned. "You're dead. Better go back to fifty pounds. I'm up over two hundred myself."

Brooks sat up and narrowed his eyebrows. "Since when are you handling that kind of weight?"

Melissa shrugged and stared up at the ceiling. "Since a week ago. You give, don't you?"

"Yeah, I give, Mel," Brooks said quietly. "Looks like you're spending a lot of time in training."

"Sure," Melissa said easily, sitting up and slinging her leg over the bench. "Better than spending my time sitting around."

Brooks looked down at the toe of his running shoe. He could hear the collective grunts of the other athletes in the background. "Look, Melissa. I know we've never really talked about what happened—"

"Forget it," Melissa interrupted.

He shook his head, trying desperately to keep his thoughts straight under Melissa's hard stare. It seemed impossible that Melissa and Faith had been the two most important women in his life. They were complete opposites. Faith always made him believe in himself. Melissa made him feel like he couldn't believe in anything ever again.

"I know I was unfair to you, Mel. I've got to explain."

"Don't bother. It's not important anymore."

Brooks looked up, stung. "But Mel, don't you want to talk about it at all?

"Nope," Melissa shot back, slinging her towel around her neck again.

"What about the appointment I made for you with the counselor?" Brooks asked shyly. "Did . . . did that work out?"

Melissa let out a short laugh. "Why should you care?"

Brooks's mouth dropped open. "I do care. I've always cared." His eyes darted around the weight room. Melissa's remarks were so loud, they were beginning to get curious stares from the other weight lifters in the room.

Melissa stood up and jammed one hand into her hip. "If you care so much about me, why did you wait until I was standing at the altar in my *wedding gown* to call the marriage off?" she blazed.

"Melissa," Brooks whispered, his eyes darting to the people who were openly staring at them now.

"If you care so much, why did you leave town right after that and refuse to speak to me?" Melissa continued to rant. "You don't care about me, Brooks Baldwin. You care only about yourself. Thank god I didn't marry you."

Brooks couldn't unglue his eyes from her twisted, angry face. In the background he could hear a few weights start to crank up again quietly. "Melissa. I'm sorry. I really feel terrible. So guilty."

"Why?" Melissa snapped back. "Why do you feel so guilty, Brooks? Why do I deserve your guilty, patronizing expressions of concern? Why are you suddenly so interested in what happens to me?"

Brooks opened his mouth to reply, but the words stuck in his throat.

Melissa drew her face closer to Brooks. "Maybe there's a reason you feel so guilty."

"What?" Brooks stood up, his heart quickening, trying to ignore the stare of a passing member of his soccer team. What was Melissa talking about?

"I think you know," Melissa tossed back over her shoulder as she began to saunter out of the weight room.

Brooks took a deep breath. Did Melissa know that he'd seen Faith the night before the wedding? Did she know about the long talk, the brief farewell kiss? Was Melissa sure about something he couldn't even settle in his own mind?

That he never got over Faith?

# Six

**B**ernie Greenberg's letter had asked Liza to be in his Hollywood office suite at three o'clock Tuesday afternoon. When the yellow taxicab swung up to the tall office building ringed by palm trees and flowering shrubs, she still had five minutes.

"Perfect," Liza breathed, checking her face one last time in her compact.

"Ten-fifty," the taxi driver grunted.

"Outrageous!" Liza cried out.

The driver looked back sourly. "What?"

Liza gave him a dazzling smile and jabbed a ten and a five into his fist. "Just kidding, hon."

The driver rolled his eyes, taking the bills.

"Keep the change, fella." Liza grinned, snapping her fake lizard purse shut.

"Gee, thanks."

"And I want you to take a look at this face," Liza straightened her back, watching as the driver turned his head around slowly. A pencil was stuck behind his ear and his graying hair was slicked back. "That's right. Take a good look."

"Okay. I looked."

"This face"—Liza touched her chin with a shiny orange nail—"is a face you're gonna see again. Soon. On television. On magazine covers. Everywhere."

"Really."

"Yeah," Liza said lightly, opening the door. "So, like I said, keep the change. There's a lot more where that came from."

Stepping out onto the steamy sidewalk, Liza watched the beat-up taxi roar off in a cloud of black exhaust. "Actually," she muttered, "I don't have it *yet*. In fact, I now have exactly twelve dollars and sixty cents to last me for the rest of the week. But that's show business." She brightened. "At least Travis will be picking me up."

Liza headed confidently toward the classy stucco-front building where Bernie Greenberg Productions was located.

In a few short days, after the obligatory screen tests

and the required meetings with directors and producers, Liza was certain she'd be walking out of here with a fat contract in her hand. Then she'd return victorious to the U. of S. and all her drama department friends would know that she wasn't kidding. That she wasn't just a blabbering fool, like they thought she was.

Liza sighed with pure happiness as she walked up the steps to the main door. She already loved everything about Hollywood. She loved the small pink fountain near the front steps. She loved the palm trees waving softly, and the way everyone seemed to be wearing or driving something white. She even loved the smog.

Liza ran a hand carefully over her sprayed hair. She even liked the way her skintight red leather skirt and splashy off-the-shoulder top seemed to blend in with the general atmosphere of the place. L.A. was like a huge carnival. A brightly lit movie set that people lived in every day.

And she was ready to move right in.

After the elevator doors opened on the building's fifth floor, Liza walked down the quiet hallway until she reached a glass door that read: BERNIE GREENBERG PRODUCTIONS.

*Head up. Big smile,* a voice inside her was singing. *You are a star and you know it. Soon the whole world is going to know it, too.*

Liza pushed open the door and stepped in with

confidence. She felt her excitement rise as she looked around the huge, tastefully decorated reception area. A thick carpet covered the floor and comfortable-looking white couches ran along three walls, facing a large table, decorated with an offbeat desert flower arrangement. A half-dozen young women were seated quietly on the couches, most of them reading scripts or flipping through *Variety*, the newspaper of the entertainment industry. Above their heads were rows of framed posters publicizing several popular television shows, probably all produced by Rich's dad, Liza guessed.

"Yes, her agent called and we have her coming in at four," a woman with white-blond hair behind the reception desk was saying in a clipped British accent.

Liza caught her eye when she put the phone down, smiled, and wiggled her fingers in greeting before settling into a prominent spot on the couch. *She knows who I am,* Liza thought to herself, hearing the satisfying creak of her hip leather skirt. *That's the way things work around here. Old Bernie probably told her to look out for the red-headed bombshell at three o'clock.*

Liza turned and looked around at all the aspiring actresses trying to look good on the couch. "Hi," she said, leaning over to a girl sitting nearest her. The girl had long black hair and was bent intently over a script.

Looking up, the girl stared at her.

"Are you here for 'Greasy Spoon'?"

The girl's shiny lips pursed. "Greasy what?"

Liza heart jumped. She hadn't even heard of it! Bernie Greenberg probably wasn't bothering to call anyone else in for an audition. "It's a new sitcom Mr. Greenberg is producing for the fall season," Liza said with a knowing smile. She even felt a little guilty. After all, this girl was probably one of a hundred unconnected hopefuls Bernie Greenberg rejected every day.

Liza ran a fingernail delicately under her hairline and looked up at the ceiling proudly. She, on the other hand, was an established, award-winning comedienne who'd already had a spot on a national cable comedy show. Even if she fell on her face in Mr. Greenberg's office, she would still have a huge advantage over everyone else in the room.

It was a sure thing.

Bernie was already crazy about her. She knew it.

After a few minutes of silence Liza stood up and walked over to the receptionist, just to make sure everyone knew she was there.

"Hi," she said brightly.

The receptionist's blue eyes opened wide and drifted down Liza's body. Liza thought her hair was windblown at first, but on closer inspection she could see it was actually a carefully styled and sprayed invention. It almost looked as if a fan were blowing her hair around her turquoise eyes, bronzed face, and wet-looking lips.

"Uh . . . hello?" Liza said again. "If you like my outfit so much I could lend it to you."

"Oh, excuse me," the receptionist said politely, though Liza thought she detected the barest hint of a smirk in the corner of her mouth. Her hot pink man's shirt had a stiff collar that flipped up. Liza could see that it tucked into a pair of black leggings that hugged her compact body. "Is there something I can help you with?"

"Yes, there is," Liza replied. "I'm Liza Ruff."

"Hi."

"Uh, right," Liza continued, reminding herself that even stars had to remain calm and patient at times. "Liza Ruff. As in meeting with Mr. Greenberg at three? I have an interview and a screen test for 'Greasy Spoon'?"

The receptionist looked beautifully confused.

"'Greasy Spoon,'" Liza repeated.

"'Greasy Spoon,'" the receptionist echoed with a blank look.

Liza leaned forward confidentially and nestled the side of her hip on the edge of the desk. "Look, I can see that not too many people are supposed to know about it. But Mr. Greenberg has seen my work and asked me to fly here."

The receptionist glared at Liza's hip, then shook her head. "Look . . . um . . . Liza," she began firmly. "Mr. Greenberg has not spoken to me about you. And I know nothing of a show called 'Greasy Spoon.'"

"Okay!" Liza burst out, her stomach starting to churn. She looked behind her furtively and lowered her voice. "Okay," she whispered. Her palms were sweating now and her pulse was throbbing in her throat. She was afraid she wouldn't be able to keep her voice steady.

"I'm really sorry . . ." the receptionist began, placing her hands on the desk and starting to get up.

Quickly, Liza unzipped her purse and drew out the letter Rich's father had sent her the week before. "Would you please look at this?" she barked.

The receptionist thumped back down in her chair.

"Mr. Greenberg's letter," Liza hissed softly. "Telling me what a great sense of humor I have. Inviting me to L.A. Telling me when my audition is."

*Dear Miss Ruff,* Liza silently recited the words she'd memorized. *Let me take this opportunity to tell you how much I enjoyed your act on the national "Laugh . . . or Else" program this week. To be frank, I am now casting the lead for a new comedy show and would be interested in having you come and test for it.*

Taking the letter, the receptionist glanced over its contents, then slowly turned it over, as if there was something on it that made her suddenly curious. "Excuse me," she said quietly, still staring down at the letter as she got up and headed into an inner office.

Liza stormed back to the couch and flopped down,

her eyes beginning to get hot with oncoming tears. Why didn't the office have her name? Why didn't the receptionist know about the show? It was probably all a mistake, she was sure. But, still, it was terribly nerve-racking.

Biting back her tears, Liza crossed her legs and waited. A few minutes later the receptionist returned and sat down next to her on the couch.

"I'm afraid there's been a little misunderstanding," she said with a mysterious smile, handing the letter back to Liza.

Liza stared at the letter, then at the receptionist. "What?"

The receptionist looked sympathetic. "I . . ."

"What?" Liza repeated. She clutched the letter to her chest. Her heart zoomed up to her throat as the receptionist's words sank in.

Gently, the receptionist put a hand on Liza's shoulder.

"Oh, my God. Oh, my God," was all Liza could say. "Do you know how far I've come? Do you have any idea . . . ?"

"Mr. Greenberg wants very much to meet with you."

Liza looked up. "He does?"

"Can you come back in two days?"

*"Two days?"* Liza moaned.

"That's when Mr. Greenberg will be back from an important shoot in Carmel. He has to leave after his next appointment." The receptionist looked sympathetically at Liza. "Thursday? Ten A.M.?"

"Fine," Liza stood up, gripping her purse. She gave Mr. Greenberg's office door one last longing glance. "Just tell him that this matter is extremely urgent. And I won't be in town for much longer. I'm staying at the Tropicana Motel if he needs to reach me."

The receptionist gave her a warm smile. "We'll be seeing you Thursday, then."

By the time Liza reached the plaza outside the building, she'd calmed down a little. "We'll be seeing you then," she muttered. She found a bench to sit down on and stared out at the Sunset Boulevard traffic.

"Okay," Liza continued to talk softly to herself. "The bottom line is—he wants me back."

A long, white limousine swooped by. Cars honked. Palm trees waved lazily in the brown sky.

Liza recrossed her legs. She didn't understand why Rich's dad had made an appointment he couldn't keep. "He's an incredibly important guy. Something must have come up," she whispered into her purse.

Standing up, Liza began to pace in front of the building, trying to ignore the rip in her panty hose she could see emerging from the toe of her shoe. "Still," she thought. "Two more nights at fifty bucks a night, not including meals? You call that soon? I call that *forever.*"

Liza checked her watch. Three-fifteen. Travis had

promised to pick her up at four. She sat down, feeling her legs begin to sweat under her leather skirt. Her panty hose were digging into her soft waist. *What we won't do for stardom,* she thought.

After forty-five minutes had passed she began searching for a sign of Travis's car. But all she could see were a thousand strangers sitting alone in a thousand separate cars, practically all of them talking on their car phones.

Liza stood up.

*This isn't so bad. I'll call his car,* she thought. *He'll pick me up, and I'll have two days to get to know him. What's bad about that?*

Liza walked briskly back into the lobby of the building and pulled a slip of paper out of her purse. She dialed Travis's number. No answer.

"Hey," Liza said to herself quietly. "You can handle this. In forty-eight hours you'll be talking to Bernie. You'll get the part. Then you'll look back at this day and laugh."

She looked up the Boulevard. Her motel was probably three or four miles away, but it was on the same street. Maybe she should just walk and save the cab fare. People in New York did it all the time.

Her spirits lifting, Liza stepped down to the sidewalk and headed east.

"I love it," Liza whistled under her breath, though the sun was beating down on her head and the exhaust fumes were starting to fill her lungs. The street was packed with honking cars, but there were hardly any people actually walking. The concrete began to burn through the soles of her high-heeled shoes.

"Hey, baby," she heard a guy yell from a passing convertible. The farther up the street she walked, the more forbidding it began to look. Now most of the businesses were adult bookstores, record stores, cheap bars, and tacky movie houses with nude shows.

"Please get me out of here," Liza finally moaned to herself as she stopped at an intersection. To her left she heard a loud, deep thumping sound, which she finally realized was a stereo system turned up full blast inside a shiny sedan with tinted windows. As Liza looked casually over, one of the car windows rolled down and the vibration suddenly turned to ear-splitting rock music.

"Yo, baby." A guy wearing a cap looked her up and down. "Come for a ride with us?"

Whistles and catcalls came from the cars. Tears were beginning to flood her eyes. But Liza knew she didn't have much choice.

All she could do was look straight ahead, steel her nerves, and hope that nothing terrible happened to her in the next two days.

# Seven

er room key was lost. Her head hurt. Her stomach growled. And her time was running out.

Faith slung her book bag wearily over her shoulder and headed out of her Wednesday morning Stagecraft class into the crowded hallway.

"Hey, Faith." Her friend Meredith playfully bumped shoulders with her. "Let's grab a cup of coffee at the student union. Got your presentation ready for the Theater Program?"

"Hi, Faith." A girl from her Stagecraft class ducked over. "What's your *Shrew* concept? I'm doing a 1950s suburb."

"I'm setting it on a pirate ship," someone called out.

"Really? I'm doing a spaceship careening through space," another added with a giggle.

"Mine's set on Wall Street."

Faith looked back at Meredith and gave him a tired smile. "No, I don't have my idea yet. And I'm up to my neck in a million other things. I'll have to pass on the coffee."

"Toodles then." Meredith gave her a comforting pat on the back before disappearing into the crowd. "Remember. We all love you."

Faith pushed through the double doors of the ancient theater arts building and stepped out into the warm spring sunshine. *Right,* Faith thought miserably as she headed for her dorm. *Everybody loves me.*

"Ouch!" she cried out as she reached the Coleridge Hall front door and caught the inside of her ankle on it. Tears flooded her eyes, but she marched determinedly up the staircase. She had to finish studying for her Western Civ test the next morning. And she had to come up with an original idea for her presentation.

As usual, the hallway in the dorm was filled with noise and confusion. The Coed-by-Bed experiment had made things even noisier. Between the spaced-out guys jamming on the saxophone in the snack room and two Coed-by-Bed experiment roommates arguing at the top of their lungs in front of the soda machine, the place was a madhouse.

"FAITH!" a familiar voice called out just as Faith managed to weave her way through the crowd to reach her door. "FAITH CROWLEY, TELEPHONE!"

Faith hesitated. Then she turned around and looked at her next-door neighbor, Kimberly Dayton, at the end of the hall, wildly waving the receiver. "Okay." Faith headed stone-faced toward the other end of the hall and took the phone from Kimberly.

"Hello?"

"Faith?" she heard Winnie's voice.

"Winnie? Is that you?" All she could hear were muffled sobs and shuffling on the other end of the line. "Winnie? What is it?"

"Faith," Winnie sobbed into the phone. "I've been trying to talk to you for days. But all I ever get is that awful Becker. I absolutely have to see you right now."

Faith planted a hand on her hip. She could hear Winnie sniffing and blowing her nose in the background. "Now?" Faith sighed.

"Y-yes. Oh please, Faith," she heard Winnie stammering and gulping for air. "I need to talk. Please come with me to the Beanery for just an hour or so. Please. Please. I'll pick you up in ten minutes."

Faith nervously twisted the telephone cord and tried to think. Winnie was one of her best friends and it sounded like she was in real trouble. But Faith absolutely couldn't talk to her right now. If she didn't get a block of time, she'd never get through her exam. And she'd miss her chance at the Professional Theater Program.

"Look, Winnie." Faith tried to stay calm. "I can't talk right now. I'm in a jam."

There was a moment of silence on the other end of the line. "I can't believe this, Faith—" Winnie sobbed.

"Winnie," Faith stopped her. "I will call you. But I can't talk now." She hung up the receiver, hating herself.

Storming back down the hall, Faith fought back the urge to scream. Everything was beginning to drive her crazy. Her friends. Her classes. Her ankle. Winnie. And most of all, herself.

She was good old Faith. Always there for everyone. Always coming through. No matter what. Never taking time for herself. Always be in the background, propping up her friends. Propping up the actors. Propping up the sets. Propping up everything and everyone until she dropped. Poor Faith.

When she tried the door, she breathed a small sigh of relief. At least it was open. She wouldn't have to scramble around to replace her key.

"Winnie," Faith muttered to herself in the semi-darkness. At least her new roommate had the good sense to close the drapes to keep the room from heating up. The room was cool and dark and blessedly quiet. "Winnie's always pushing, always needing, always in the middle of some crisis. And she's married now! Where is Josh?"

Slamming her book bag down on her dresser, she looked at her tired face in the mirror. Then she looked at the message from Lauren, still stuck in the mirror frame. "Lauren wants to talk. Winnie wants to talk. What's the matter with everyone? Don't they realize I have a life, too? Or do I?"

Faith swung around. She was about to dive onto her bed, then froze, horrified.

Becker was there.

He'd heard every word.

Sitting cross-legged in the corner of the room, Becker was wearing a pair of shorts and a loose-fitting white T-shirt. "Oh," Faith murmured, her face getting hot with embarrassment. She felt so stupid and mean. Becker must think she'd totally lost it.

She stared self-consciously as Becker's eyes opened slowly. Quietly, he unhooked his legs and rolled his shoulders. Then he looked straight at her. "I'm sorry," he said, serious. He was like a cool, calm oasis in the middle of her crazy circle of agitated friends. "Did I surprise you?"

Embarrassed, she drew her hands up to her face. "No, *I'm* sorry. Is this when you . . . uh . . . meditate?"

"Yes." Becker smiled. "And now I'm done."

"Looks relaxing," Faith said, not knowing what else to say. "A lot of people I know in the theater do it before a show."

"That makes sense."

The sound of muffled laughter and ringing telephones vibrated through the door. Inside the peaceful room with Becker, all was calm. Slowly, Faith dropped her hands and sat down on her bed.

"You must think I'm crazy, talking to myself like that." Faith closed her eyes. There was something cool and removed about Becker that made her feel as if she could say anything.

"Of course you're not crazy."

Faith opened her eyes and looked down at him. She blushed. "I . . . guess I was just blowing off a little steam."

"Pure experience," Becker said cheerfully.

"Pure what?"

"Pure experience," Becker repeated, standing up and flopping back on the bed opposite hers. "That's what the American philosopher William James called it. Freud would call it the rising of your unconscious thoughts into your conscious mind."

"Oh."

"Anyway, it was real, Faith," Becker said with a warm smile. "Don't ignore it. You said your friends need you too much. That they don't understand you have a life of your own. Pay attention to your feelings. That's your truth."

Faith gave Becker a weak smile. "I've been a little testy with my friends lately. It's just that I've been under so much pressure. And I've been terrified about my presentation."

"You said you wanted your life back," Becker said, slipping on his glasses. "Is that so much to ask of your friends?"

"Look," Faith began, biting her lip and fiddling with the collar on her blouse. "My friends are important to me. I mean, I can't just live my life alone. I have to have time for them."

Becker's blue eyes were staring at her softly. "This may sound a little too philosophical for you right now. I mean, I know you're upset. But this is what Joseph Campbell said. He was an amazing philosopher and mythologist. He said you can't save the world until you save yourself."

Faith cleared her throat. "You make it sound like I'm drowning or something."

Becker looked at Faith with understanding and sympathy. "But don't you see?" he said patiently. "You *are*. You are an artist, Faith. It's your path—your responsibility—to focus on your art. But your creative energy is being drained by your well-meaning friends."

"I think you're right," Faith reflected. She couldn't imagine Becker calling her up at all hours, begging her to talk. He was so different. So at peace. It made her want to get closer to whatever it was he had.

Becker lowered his eyes and smiled. "I don't have a lot of friends, that's true. But I've kept the really important ones."

Faith gave him a small smile. "It works for you, huh?"

Becker nodded slowly, his hands still relaxed at his sides, his long, well-shaped face and rugged, smoothly shaved chin making him look older than a college student. "Focus."

"Focus," Faith echoed, staring at him, transfixed.

"Focus is everything," Becker continued. His voice was deep and steady. "It's the only reason I have a 3.9 grade point average, for example. I know how to channel my energies by organizing my time, limiting the number of people I see, and concentrating."

Faith shook her head in frustration, then sank her head in her hands. "I'll never focus. If you could look inside my mind right now, you'd see a three-ring circus." She snapped her head back up in anger and could feel hot tears behind her eyes. "The more I try to think of an idea for *Taming of the Shrew,* the more blocked I get."

There was a long silence in the dim room. Faith stared straight ahead into space, panicked. For a moment she felt a strange falling sensation, as if the bottom were dropping out of her life, taking her down with it.

Then, just as quickly, something caught her. She looked down. It was Becker's hand slipping into hers.

"Becker?"

"Come on, Faith." Becker was kneeling on the floor below her. "I'll show you what I do every day to relax. It's not difficult."

Faith hesitated. Then she slid down onto the floor

next to Becker and crossed her legs. After all, what did she have to lose?

"Start by closing your eyes and taking slow deep breaths," Becker instructed. "And don't laugh. Whatever you do, don't laugh."

Faith began to giggle, then forced herself to stop. Slowly she drew in a breath, and let it out easily.

"That's good," she heard Becker say close to her ear. Already she was beginning to feel a little calmer. Outside, she could hear a door slam and someone yelling in the bathroom. But she was starting to block it all out.

"Now try this," Becker continued. "Don't laugh now. It's an ancient Tibetan chant." Faith could feel Becker settling into position. Then she heard a strange sound coming from his throat. *"AUM,"* Becker sang in a low, melodic tone. *"A—U—M,"* he chanted.

"Mmmmm." Faith listened. "Interesting."

"Try it," Becker urged. "It's the sound of the energy of the universe. You start in the back of your mouth. *Ahhhh,*" he demonstrated. "Then you move the sound forward. *Ooooooooo.* Then *mmmmmm.* You close the mouth. Try imagining all the vowels in one smooth sound."

*"Aaaa–uuuuuu–mmmmm,"* Faith chanted. *"Aaaaaa–uuuuuu–mmmmmmmmm."*

"Good," Becker whispered into her ear, tickling it a little. "It rises out of the silence, then descends back again."

*"Aaaaa–uuuuu–mmmm,"* Faith couldn't resist repeating. She felt all her muscles begin to relax as she imagined the delicious, calming image of sound rising and falling like an ocean wave.

"You're very good at this, Faith," Becker said quietly. "If you don't look out you're going to end up with a shaved head in a Tibetan monastery."

Faith giggled.

"Hey, wait!" Becker joked. "This is serious. You're not supposed to laugh. This is very, very, very serious aaauummming." Becker began to laugh, too.

*"Aaauummm."* Faith broke off with a loud snort, unable to remain serious. She hadn't felt so good all week.

"Come on now," Becker joked, beginning to tickle her. "Serious. Serious."

Tears rolled down Faith's cheeks as she shrieked with delight. Quickly she reached for Becker's stomach and began tickling him back. Within a few moments, Faith and Becker were a rolling mass of hysterical giggling on the dorm room floor.

*KNOCK. KNOCK. KNOCK.*

"There's someone at the door," Becker said, lunging for Faith's ribs again.

*"AAAAHHHHH!"* Faith screamed.

"Faith?" a deep voice called out from the hall. Then the door opened and a shaft of light fell into the room. Faith looked up.

It was Brooks.

Faith looked at him, still convulsed with giggles. He was frowning down at her, his fists stuffed into his rugby shorts and his muscular legs planted firmly in place. Faith knew that look. She knew that way he stood. Solid, patient Brooks. He always used to stand that way when something really, really annoyed him.

"Faith?" Brooks repeated stiffly.

"Hi, Brooks." Faith giggled as Becker pulled away and leaned back casually on one hand. "What are you doing here?"

Brooks bristled, but it was obvious he was trying to be patient. "I needed to talk to you."

Faith tried to compose herself. A loud snort escaped suddenly, causing her to start giggling again. "Becker's teaching me how to meditate."

"That's great." Brooks stared suspiciously at Becker. He hiked his book bag up on his shoulder, then extended his hand. "Becker? I'm Brooks Baldwin."

"Oh," Faith said softly. "Sorry. Becker and I are part of the Coed-by-Bed experiment."

"Oh." Brooks relaxed his shoulders a little. There was an awkward silence as Faith and Becker stared up at Brooks. "So, do you have a minute, Faith?" Brooks was pursing his lips and looking very tense.

"Oh," Faith said, her heart sinking. Someone *else* needed to talk? Maybe she needed to set up a public confessional booth.

"Look," Brooks said, his eyes darting nervously in Becker's direction. "I'm sorry I walked in. But I need to talk with you, Faith. Soon. Something's come up with Melissa."

"Brooks," Faith protested. "I just can't right now."

Brooks had a pleading look in his eyes. "Please, Faith. Meet me tonight somewhere."

"She's got a Western Civ exam at ten o'clock and needs to study for it," Becker spoke up.

Brooks's mouth dropped open in disbelief. He looked from Faith to Becker and back again. "Look, pal. Faith and I go way back. And I'd like to speak with her."

"Faith . . ." Becker began.

Brooks looked angry. "Who is this guy, Faith? Your babysitter?"

Becker stood up and met Brooks's angry gaze.

Slowly, Faith stood up. "Becker's right, Brooks. I can't meet you tonight. It's not just the huge exam tomorrow. It's everything."

Brooks shook his head. "I don't believe this. I was always there for you, Faith. Always."

Faith felt a thread of guilt beginning to wind its way through her heart. Brooks was right. In the four years they'd gone together, never once did he turn away when she needed him. "Okay," Faith said suddenly. "I will meet you at eight tonight. But only for a little while."

Brooks sighed with relief. "Thanks. How's the OK Cafe? It's downtown. Can you get there?"

"Yes," Faith said. If she left the cafe by nine-thirty, she'd have the rest of the night to study and the rest of the day after the exam for *Shrew*.

"I knew you'd come through." Brooks breathed easier as he closed the door behind him.

"I'm worried about you," Becker said, calmly tying his sneakers. "Your friends are eating you alive."

"He's one of my oldest friends," Faith tried to explain. "We went together for years and he's trying to get over a broken engagement."

Becker stood up and looked at her seriously. "But you're in trouble, too. You told him that, didn't you?"

"Yes."

"So whose troubles did he think were more important?" Becker asked. "Yours or his?"

"His."

"Right."

"But I couldn't just stand there and say no. I had to take some kind of action," Faith pleaded.

"For every action there's an equal but opposite reaction," Becker stated.

"Sir Isaac Newton," Faith said with a grin.

"Very good, Faith." Becker nodded. "You're a good student."

"I have a good teacher," Faith deadpanned as she lunged to tickle him some more.

# Eight

"*B*efore I introduce you to the thumb gouge, scratch, and elbow jab techniques," Lauren's self-defense teacher was saying, "I'd like to spend a few moments on our basic defensive stance."

Lauren placed her left foot forward, bent her knees, and raised her right fist up from her bent elbow. She clenched the other fist near her waist and gave the bare wall a menacing glare.

"Come on, everyone," the instructor yelled. "Repeat after me: I AM POWERFUL!"

"*I AM POWERFUL!*" The voices of thirty women echoed off the walls of the U. of S. Women's Center.

Lauren grinned. Her round face was flushed with excitement and her outstretched thigh felt slim and powerful. Since arriving on campus last fall as a frightened, overweight sorority mouse, her life had taken a 180° turn. In a few short months, she'd slimmed down, challenged her wealthy, overbearing parents, and become one of the hottest writers on the campus newspaper. At last she was thinking and acting for herself. Without leaning on anyone.

Including Dash Ramirez.

On top of everything else, her self-defense class was giving her an even stronger sense of empowerment. Nothing was going to stop her now.

Her instructor, Deborah Ratan, gave the group an enthusiastic smile, and flipped her long, dark ponytail behind her. "Learning to defend yourself is a powerful choice. When we act with dignity and power— whether we're being threatened physically, or simply responding to daily challenges— we are no longer victims. We are powerful women."

Lauren joined the enthusiastic applause and hugged the woman who was standing next to her.

"Okay," Deborah shouted. "Defensive stance. Focus everyone!"

Lauren focused.

"Come on!" Deborah shouted. "Focus on your center. Focus on the rage every woman feels in the face of her oppressor. Focus on the anger within you."

Lauren gritted her teeth. She was angry all right. For too long, she'd let everyone be her oppressor. Not just men. Her parents. Her teachers. Her so-called friends at the fancy boarding schools. Dash Ramirez. And now Melissa. At last she was throwing off the chains.

"Okay, class," Deborah called out. "Over to the wall pillows. Basic kneeling punch position!"

Lauren strode over to the pillow area, clenched her fist and threw several right and left punches into a sofa cushion.

"On guard every minute," Deborah shouted over the grunting line of women. "Self-defense must be second-nature, not just a clever technique we think we can pull out of a hat when we're physically threatened. In a real attack, there won't be time to remember specific moves—or to think at all. We'll have to go on instinct."

"Yeah," Lauren whispered to herself as she gave the pillow another powerful punch.

"Keep the fist tight and the wrist straight, everyone! Let your elbow drive the fist forward. Remember, a good strike must be executed quickly, preferably to the eyes, nose, throat, or groin."

Lauren stopped briefly to examine her sore knuckles. As she did, she noticed someone familiar on the sidelines of the large room. She turned and their eyes connected.

It was Dash.

Dropping her eyes down, she tried to regain her balance. There was something about Dash that always made her knees buckle a little and sent annoying prickles all over her scalp. Wearing faded jeans and a ripped sweatshirt, he looked like his usual self. Except that he looked a little paler and a little more tired than usual. His scraggly, dark hair hung down around his collar and it looked as if he hadn't shaved in three or four days.

Desperately, she tried to focus her anger at Dash.

*Pow!* She tried to hate the way his large, dark eyes seemed to follow her everywhere these days, waiting to trap her in his puppy dog gaze.

*Crack!* She reminded herself of what Dash had put her through months before. The paralyzing shock of being dumped without warning. The horrible sadness and depression that followed. The confusing signals about getting back together, followed by his relationship with sorority princess Courtney Conner. It was incredible. Even after he vowed to forget Courtney, he went to extraordinary lengths to take her side in the sexual harassment charge.

"Take a break. Five minutes," Deborah yelled. "Then we'll work on groin chops, pinches, and ear twists."

"Hi," Lauren heard Dash's voice behind her. "Melissa said I could find you here. I hope you don't mind."

Lauren swung around and stared into Dash's pale, handsome face. He stood with his arms hanging limply at his sides, a manila folder in one hand. "Actually, I *do* mind. You're breaking my concentration."

"Okay," Dash replied with a deep, apologetic sigh, not taking his eyes off her. Then he backed away a little, as if he were waiting for her to kick him out. In the background, the sounds of punches and ear-splitting self-defense screams continued, but Dash seemed unaware of them.

Lauren softened and stepped forward. "What is it, Dash?"

"Our 'His/Her' column for the *Journal* on Courtney's sexual harassment case is due tomorrow," Dash said anxiously. "But I've got a thirty-inch political piece I've got to write tonight. This is the only time I have to go over the column with you."

"Okay, shoot," Lauren said, impatiently running a hand through her curly hair. "I read your half last night."

"Um," Dash began, awkwardly pulling out copies of both their contributions. "What can I say? Your piece was intelligent and tightly written. I'm glad you didn't take Courtney's side on this issue. The boy-versus-girl thing would have been too predictable."

"Oh, really?" Lauren replied, tilting her head to the side.

"Yeah. Now, tell me what you thought of my piece," Dash said slowly, "I can take it."

"Well, Dash," Lauren said, taking his copy and sliding her back down the wall until she was sitting. She flipped through several pages, then looked up at him casually. "I thought it could use about ten hours of rewrite."

"What?"

"The thrust of your argument—basically praising women who have the guts to complain about creeps who harass them—was okay, I guess."

"You guess?"

"But you're getting lazy, Ramirez." Lauren looked at Dash's stunned face. "You have too many run-on sentences, clichés, misspelled words. Your grammar is terrible. Plus, you have a sort of tired way of making each point. Put some zip into it."

"Gee, thanks a lot, Lauren," Dash snapped loudly, attracting several glares from the other women in the class. "I'll try to keep all that in mind."

"Good," Lauren said irritably. "Dash, you're the one who always urged me to be tough. Didn't you think it would ever come back to you?

Dash placed a hand on his hip and planted a challenging foot forward. "While we're on the subject of our personal writing habits," his voice rose again. "If this needs so much rewriting, then let me tell you what *you* can do tonight."

"What's that?" Lauren stuck her chin out defiantly.

"Spend some time cleaning up your arrogant, oh-so-serious-and-above-it all tone," Dash spat. "We're all with you politically, Lauren. It's not like you discovered feminism. It's the nineties. You're a feminist. I'm a feminist. Ninety-five percent of the campus agrees with you. Okay?"

Lauren's eyes were burning. "You . . . are . . . so . . . wrong."

Dash was nodding rapidly, his face tense. "Oh, yeah. As usual. Lauren's right. Dash is wrong."

"You have no idea what women go through," Lauren practically screamed. Dash had no idea. He never did. He was just like all men. Selfish, insensitive, and incapable of facing reality.

"I know what you do, Lauren," Dash whispered hoarsely. The entire self-defense class was staring at them openly now. "You spend a lot of time building walls and shutting yourself off. First it was your damn shyness. Then it was your fear of failure. And now it's just plain anger. Useless, stupid, stubborn anger."

"Thanks a lot, doctor," Lauren hissed back, throwing the pages of Dash's column in his face. "Now why don't you just go back to sorority row and find someone else to analyze?"

"I think I will," Dash replied bitterly, scooping the papers off the floor. "I was going to walk you home after your class. Something made me remember how much you hated walking by the Pioneer Graveyard by yourself at night."

Lauren bit her lip.

"But now I know you'll be just fine," Dash said in a low voice. "If a mugger jumps out at you, you can just go ahead and beat the crap out of him. After all, I wouldn't want to insult you by actually offering to help."

That was the trouble with Dash, Lauren thought bitterly. He always knew how to hurt her. And he didn't hesitate to. He knew which buttons to press. It made her feel alone and defenseless. There didn't seem to be anywhere to turn. Anyone to talk to.

*Faith! Help!*

Faith stepped off a downtown Springfield bus and headed rapidly down a dimly lit sidewalk toward the OK Cafe. Up ahead, she could see its flashing, neon sign.

Smoothing back a few stray hairs, she rushed trying not to think about the precious study time that was ticking away. Brooks had seemed so upset about Melissa that afternoon. It was impossible for her to turn her back to him.

After all, this was Brooks. Her ex. Her high school sweetheart for four years. The person she probably knew better than anyone else in the world. Or at least used to.

Suddenly Faith realized that she'd reached the front entrance.

From the sidewalk, she could hear throbbing dance

music and wild laughter. As the door kept opening and closing, she could see hip-looking couples in leather jackets and expensive-looking haircuts.

Slowly, Faith looked down at her own frayed jeans, oversized sweatshirt, and cowboy boots. "I thought this was going to be a divy downtown cafe," she muttered. Shrugging wearily, Faith pushed open the shiny red door. Making her way through the front filled with noisy partiers in their early twenties, Faith could hardly believe steady, conservative Brooks had picked this place for a quiet chat.

*I've got work to do, Brooks,* Faith thought irritably, searching for his familiar head of blond curls. *Why are you dragging me away from studying? I don't have time to party.*

"Faith!" she heard her name being called. A moment later she felt Brooks's hand on her shoulder, guiding her. After wandering for a few minutes through the flashing lights and hurrying waitresses, Brooks finally settled her into a quiet table in the back of the room.

"Two Cokes and some fries," Brooks called out to a young woman carrying a tray of drinks.

Faith slid behind the table and stared at the dance floor which was packed with expensive clothes and athletic-looking bodies. "This is where you wanted to talk?" Faith said, moving closer to Brooks so he could hear her. "Listen. I can't stay long."

"That's okay." Brooks was bopping his head to the beat of the music, looking at her. His curly hair was shining in the glittery light. "Can you believe it, Faith? It's a nonalcoholic dance club. And you can see it's pretty popular."

Faith narrowed her eyes and looked over his outfit. She hadn't seen him wear anything but a rugby shirt or a beat-up T-shirt since the senior prom. Tonight he looked like a clothing ad for a hip and casual lifestyle. His bare forearms looked familiar and sturdy, but it looked as if he were trying to shake off his old stuffy, senior-class-president image.

Faith decided to get to the point right away. "So, what's up with Melissa? Is she okay?"

Brooks slid an elbow out onto the table and cradled the side of his face in one hand, gazing seriously at Faith. "I'm not sure."

"Well. What happened?" It seemed strange. Everything about Brooks had always been so sure, so dependable. So, well . . . the same. Now everything seemed different. "What did you want to talk with me about?"

Brooks sat up straight and folded his hands in front of him. "I saw Melissa yesterday in the weight room." He shrugged his wide shoulders. "She was the same. Angry. Unforgiving. Back into training in a big way. In fact, she seems to be doing a lot better than I am right now."

Faith sighed and glanced at her watch. "So what's the problem?"

"I finally figured out why *I'm* the one who's still suffering over this mess." Brooks leaned slightly in Faith's direction. "You see, *I'm* the one who has to deal with the guilt. Melissa gets to be the innocent victim."

"But is it really guilt you're feeling?" Faith asked. "I mean, sure, you walked out, but you had to. You knew you had to. Right?"

"Of course." Brooks nodded. His usually bright eyes looked dull, even sad. "It's guilt though. No doubt about it. Because I *am* guilty. And now I realize why. I figured it out this morning, when I saw you and Becker together."

"What?"

"The truth is, Faith," Brooks said, his voice shaking a little, "that I didn't go through with the wedding because I still felt something for you."

Faith froze.

Brooks brushed her hand with his fingertips, then quickly moved away.

Desperately, Faith looked around the room, trying to find a spot to settle her eyes and think. But everything was glittering and swirling. Everyone was laughing and dancing. She couldn't think or move or even breathe. What was Brooks saying?

She looked over, gasping, and saw that Brooks was staring forlornly into space.

"Now that I think about it," Brooks said dully, not waiting for her to answer, "it doesn't seem that strange. I mean, you and I spent four years together. Four happy years."

"Brooks, please . . ." Faith cried softly.

"After you broke things off in the fall . . . well, that's when I met Mel. And maybe I *was* trying to recreate what you and I had together. Maybe she reminded me a little of the Faith I used to know. The Faith who really appreciated me. The Faith who completely disappeared the moment we set foot on this campus."

Faith's mouth dropped open. Brooks was still upset about that? After all the months away from each other. After his relationship with Melissa and his engagement and his whole new life. He was *still angry?*

"Brooks," Faith said, her voice cracking with emotion. "I explained everything to you. You didn't want me to change or grow. You know that," she protested over the throbbing music. "You wanted little Faith to stay the same forever. Couldn't you see that you were suffocating me?"

Brooks set his jaw. "Didn't look that way to me."

Faith buried her face in her hands, her heart sinking like a lead weight. "Brooks," she moaned. "How could you take your relationship with Melissa that far without figuring it out? How could you?"

"I don't know," Brooks said miserably. "That's

why I feel so bad about this."

Faith felt a surge of anger rise up in her throat. "How could you be so completely out of touch with your feelings, Brooks? Do you know how much you've hurt Melissa?"

"Look," Brooks said hotly, "you were with me the night before the wedding. We talked. I told you about my doubts. And you let me kiss you!"

Faith gasped as the waitress set down their order. The night before the wedding, Brooks needed to talk to her. He seemed upset. She was only trying to help him, not sabotage his wedding to Melissa! "I don't believe this, Brooks." Faith breathed. "Are you actually trying to blame me for this?" Quickly, Faith glanced at her watch. She knew she had to get back to study for her Western Civ exam, but there was no way she could just let the whole thing drop. It was too important.

"Hey." Brooks shoved a french fry in his mouth and sat back in his seat. "Take off if you want, Faith. I'll just sit here and drown in my misery. Like Becker said, you've got a lot of big things going on this week. Next time I'll schedule my failures for a less busy week."

Faith stared at his stony profile, unable to move. "Brooks," she said quietly. "You have to understand that I still care very much about you."

"Uh-huh."

"But I'm not in love with you."

"That's pretty clear, Faith."

"Come on, Brooks," Faith said gently. "Talk to me. I didn't realize you were going through so much pain."

Brooks settled his gaze into space.

"Come on, Brooks," Faith tried, feeling all of a sudden like she owed this—this time—to him. Maybe she never really had explained everything to Brooks on that moonlit autumn night in her dorm room when she unexpectedly broke up with him. And maybe he'd never really had a chance to respond.

Faith sighed and stared at a young woman with a purple beehive leaving the restroom. A tray of dishes crashed nearby and the thumping music went on in the distance. But for the first time in months, Brooks was talking to her.

Faith thought back to the fall. They'd been at the U. of S. less than a week when she realized that she was desperate for change and challenge. Now she realized that Brooks had never really been equipped to handle the change. Strong, steady Brooks wanted to protect her. And perhaps he'd transferred that need to Melissa.

Faith gazed at Brooks's dependable, warm face. Was Melissa's pain actually her fault?

Slowly, carefully, Brooks began to talk about them. About Melissa. And Faith listened. It was as if they were finally far enough apart to figure out where they'd been. It wasn't easy, and it took longer than she thought it would. But suddenly, letting Brooks talk became the most important thing in the world to her.

More important that her Western Civ exam. More important that her theater program presentation.

Before long, their Cokes were gone and she and Brooks were slipping quietly out into the warm spring night.

"We missed the last bus back to campus, Faith," Brooks said wearily. "I'm sorry I kept you out so late, with your exam coming up and everything. It was selfish of me. I guess we'll have to walk back to your dorm."

Faith rubbed her eyes, drained. She hadn't said a word in hours. Brooks had done all the talking. As they drew near the campus and passed Plotsky Fountain, she realized that she'd have to be back there within a few hours, taking a major exam. And she wasn't prepared.

Brooks had picked the worst possible night to bare his soul.

And somehow she had fallen into his trap.

# *Nine*

....................

"*T*heater Arts* magazine, May 1989," Becker whispered to himself, lifting another publication off the stack with his sure, slender hand. Sitting cross-legged on the floor of Faith's dorm room, he straightened his back again and calmly took in another review. "Mmmmmm. *A Midsummer Night's Dream* as a circus with acrobats and swings."

For a moment his eyes flicked up. He listened through the usual sounds coming from the hallway. Then he checked the clock. Ten-thirty and Faith was still not back from seeing Brooks. Becker's mind rapidly analyzed the new situation. Then he smiled thoughtfully down at his neat piles of theater magazines and photocopied reviews. When it was all over, he'd be the one who got her into the theater program. While Brooks would be the one who nearly kept her out.

"Good," Becker murmured aloud into the empty room. He gazed for a few moments at Faith's bulletin board and desk, crammed with photographs, souvenirs, theater ticket stubs, piles of stuffed animals, dried up flower arrangements, wrinkled balloons left over from many parties, Post-It notes and scribbled messages. All were reminders of a life too full. Of a life that was sure to destroy her.

"Can't she see that?" Becker said, bending his head back down to his reading material. "*American Theater* magazine. July 1976. Guthrie Theater performs *The Tempest* with beatnik twist. Not Faith's style." Becker shook his head.

Then something interesting caught his eye that made even Becker's meditative heartbeat skip a little. It was a review of an old production of *Oklahoma*.

"Hmmmm." He rose and began slowly pacing the room. He thought of Faith's cowboy boots, her childhood in a small western town. Her veterinarian father.

"Faith could make that come alive," Becker whispered. "If only I knew how to make it work. *Shrew* in the wild West? Fence posts and haystacks? Fiddle music?" He smiled to himself, strode across the room, and blew out a small candle, picturing the curve of Faith's beautiful face. "Faith, you and I are going to do great things together."

Becker lay down on his spare bed and gave the ceiling a satisfied grin. He thought about his first glimpse of Faith, in the dining commons, right after Thanksgiving break.

She'd been across the room, calmly carrying a tray to an empty table, while her friends swarmed around her, all talking at once. Something about her had made him decide she would be the right one. Was it the serene look on her face? Her clear, blue eyes? A stillness within?

Becker smiled at the memory. Even from a distance he could tell how warm she was. How willing she was to give.

It was exactly what he needed.

What he'd never had growing up.

And what he'd never been able to find in a woman. Becker frowned to himself. Women were usually takers. He'd get involved and suddenly it was *their* schedule. *Their* friends. And *their* interests. He wanted someone to be with him completely. Exclusively.

The more he knew Faith, the more he knew she was right for him. He knew that he could make her his. All his.

Then the Coed-by-Bed experiment came along. It had been sponsored partly by the Psych department, where he knew the teaching assistant in charge. That connection had come in handy. He found out that Faith had signed up for it and he quietly put his name next to hers on the list.

"I'm going to show you how great your life will be without all your hangers-on. Your strange, crass, and inferior friends," Becker whispered. "You need me, Faith. You need me to save you from them. And I'll prove to you that I'm worth all of your friends put together."

Becker heard a noise outside the door and slipped the book on the desk behind his head. Quickly, he planted one foot on the floor and with one wide sweep shoved the theater reviews and magazines under the narrow bed, flicking off the light with his other hand. He slid under his blanket, listening to Faith fumble for her keys and finally open the door.

"Oh!" Becker heard her gasp as she stumbled over something near the door. For a moment, the room was quiet. He could hear her light, lovely step in the darkness. He could smell her warm flowery scent.

Slowly, Becker pretended to stir under his scratchy blanket, as if he were rousing from a deep sleep. He yawned a little, then lifted his head up. "Hi," he mumbled sleepily. "You're back."

In the darkness, Becker could barely make out Faith, who was sitting on the edge of her bed, her head in her hands. "Yeah, I'm back," she said dully. "I'm really sorry I woke you, Becker."

Becker took a breath. He could hear her gentle breathing. At last, everything was dark and quiet and peaceful. They were alone. "I don't mind."

"No, really, Becker," Faith insisted, still shaking her head and staring at the floor through her legs. "You don't understand. It's really late. You've got early classes and I've ruined it for you. I'm really sorry, especially since you're always so considerate."

Becker sat up, dressed only in a pair of track shorts. "I don't need much sleep, Faith," he said quietly, flicking on a small study light.

There was a long silence. Becker watched as Faith pushed herself back on the bed with one foot until she was leaning against the wall, looking away from him into space. Her eyes looked a little puffy and her mouth was tight and trembling. "I . . . don't . . . know . . . what . . . I'm . . . doing," Faith said softly.

Becker didn't move. His eyes were taking her in. He wanted to memorize everything about her. The way her silky hair fell down her shoulders. The curve of her lower lip. She was *the one*. The one he needed. The only one who was capable of understanding him and loving him. "What happened, Faith?" he said finally.

Faith's eyes lifted. Slowly, they slid over to the clock on her desk. "It's midnight," she said, defeated. He watched as she raked her long hair back with her fingers. "I've spent less than an hour today studying for Western Civ."

"Is there anything I can do to help?" Becker asked. He watched, breathless, as the tears began to fill her eyes.

Faith suddenly looked up and stared at him quizzically, as if she'd read his thoughts. In the dim light she looked like the kind of girl who kissed very, very softly. Whose hands were very smooth and gentle. "I can't remember the last time anyone asked me that."

Becker was thrilled.

Faith got up, crossed her arms in front of her chest, and walked to the window. "Can I help *you*, Faith? What do *you* need, Faith? Is everything okay, Faith?" She whirled around and faced him, her eyes blazing. "No one ever asks me!"

"I asked you," Becker said softly.

Faith threw her head back and let out a bitter laugh. "I know. But, with everyone else it's always, please help me, Faith. I've got to talk, Faith. I need you, Faith." She covered her face with both hands. "There's nothing left of me. Nothing."

"You can change all that," Becker murmured, gazing at her slim silhouette against the light shining up from the dorm green.

"I *am* going to change," Faith snapped back. "Take what happened tonight, for instance."

"What happened?" Becker asked.

"Brooks was desperate. He had to talk. . . ." Faith began crying softly and sat back down again. "It was so intense." She looked up at Becker, her cheeks wet. "I wanted to help. But now I see that Brooks just used me. And I'm left with nothing. The time is all gone, Becker."

"Faith . . ." Becker gently tried to interrupt. He wanted to reach out and touch her. She was so close. So ready for him to help her.

"It's useless," Faith cried out, flinging her head down on her pillow.

"Let me help."

"It's too late," Faith sobbed.

For a while, he just sat there and let her cry. Then, after a while, she looked up from her pillow and fixed her eyes intently on him. Becker felt a thrill. "Do you know what my senior class at Lewis and Clark High voted me?" she asked.

Becker smiled and shrugged. He drew his knees up and wrapped his arms around them thoughtfully. "Let me guess. Most Likely to Direct a Broadway Hit?"

Faith shook her head bitterly. "Absolutely not."

Becker hesitated, then decided to risk it. "Most Beautiful?"

Faith's face drained for a moment, then recovered. She looked over at the pom-poms pinned to her bulletin board and furrowed her brow. "Most Congenial."

Becker smiled. "Well, Faith. I've got to admit. You *are* congenial."

"It's right there in the yearbook for all to see," Faith continued, angrily pulling back her hair. "Not Most Likely to Direct on Broadway. Not Most Likely to Graduate from College Summa Cum Laude. Not even Most Likely to Do Okay."

"Congenial," Becker echoed, flexing the muscles in his arms. "What an empty sort of award to give someone like you. Weren't you already involved in the theater?"

"YES!" Faith practically screamed. "I'd been involved in the theater since my sophomore year! I even directed a scene from *Taming of the Shrew* that won first place in the Western High School Drama Festival! But all anyone could think of was: 'Wow, she's so *congenial*.'"

Becker shook his head and stared at her distraught face. "It's not too late to change. Your friends . . ."

"Don't say another word about my friends," Faith snapped. "I know they take advantage of me. I know I have to change. But it's not that easy."

Becker paused. Then he looked over at her desk. "Are those your study notes?"

Faith let out a frustrated breath. "Oh, yeah. Those are my notes all right. Sitting over there all by themselves. Stranded."

"Are you tired?"

Faith looked at him. "Come to think of it, I think I'm getting my second wind."

"Let's start, then." Becker rose and walked over to her desk. He lifted the pile of notes and selected one of her textbooks. "And let's go over this supplementary reading material in the Lavin textbook. Professor Hermann used it extensively last year in the midterm.

Faith's mouth dropped open. "You took Western Civ from Hermann last year?"

"Sure I did." Becker's smile widened.

Faith's hand rose up to her mouth. "You'd do this for me? "Sure," Becker answered, standing up, taking his blanket and spreading it out on the floor. He patted the place next to him. "Come on. We'll study until two. Then you sleep until eight, a half an hour after I leave for breakfast and my first class. Then you meditate until eight-thirty, have a decent breakfast, and take the test. You'll do fine."

Stunned, Faith quickly pulled off her boots and settled down on the floor next to him.

"Now," Becker began. "Just think of three important, intertwined issues that dominate the entire Renaissance period. . . ." he began. He let his brain go on automatic pilot so that he could focus on the fact that he was so near her. That he was helping her. And that she needed him.

"That's amazing." Faith yawned at the end of their study session, lying on her back on Becker's blanket. "How do you manage to put history into such neat little packages? It makes it so much easier to remember."

Becker rolled over on his side and propped his head up on his elbow so that he was looking down on her.

She was so close.

"And those little rhyming memory tricks you taught me," Faith mumbled sleepily. "I'm not going to forget those dates for the rest of my life."

"No," Becker whispered, lifting a strand of her hair from her arm. "You'll never forget."

Faith's eyes opened. She looked at him curiously. Tenderly, even. Then she rolled over slightly, reached out, and touched his bare arm. "I can't tell you . . . I mean . . . this really means a lot to me, Becker."

Becker opened his mouth, then closed it. He wouldn't tell her about his feelings now. Instead, he gave a half smile and brushed the side of her cheek with the back of his hand. "Any friend would have done it."

A tear rolled slowly out of Faith's eye. "I don't have any friends then, Becker. Because no one really comes through for me like this anymore."

"You have a friend now," Becker said softly, carefully, slipping his hand around her soft shoulder. "A true friend." He could feel her respond slowly by reaching her warm arm around his neck and hugging him close. He breathed in the scent of her hair. He felt the gentle shaking of her body as she cried.

Becker almost felt like crying himself. But instead, he pulled a blanket over the two of them and moved closer to her on the floor.

After a few minutes, her breathing became even and he saw that she was sound asleep. But this time, he couldn't stop himself. He lifted his head, leaned over her face, and swept his lips briefly over hers.

But she didn't awaken.

# Ten

......................

"**YEAH YEAH YEAH YEAH YEAH YEAH YEAH YEAH!**" an anguished scream came from Travis's car radio, backed by a ragged electric guitar that began buzzing crazily into the stratosphere.

"Yeah, right. What a concept," Travis muttered, abruptly turning the radio off and checking his watch. "Hey. Hire me on. You could experiment with a real songwriter. Maybe even a real song." He rubbed his eyes sleepily with one hand and felt the cool morning air rush through the window and brush against his cheek. "Seven A.M. in L.A. Show time!"

Flicking on his turn signal, Travis turned off

Fairfax Avenue onto Sunset Boulevard. Then he picked up the car phone and checked in. "Hey. This is Travis Bennett. I'm heading west for the Beverly Hills Hotel. Got anything?"

"Morning, Travis," his dispatcher said briskly. "We need a seven-fifteen pickup at the entrance, pronto. Two big shots headed for the airport. Check in with me after your drop."

"Yeah, okay," Travis answered, hanging up the phone and staring out at the huge cartoonlike billboards lining the Strip as he whizzed by. "Hello, Marlboro Man. Hello, Movie Star," he whispered. In the dim morning light he could make out a few tired people ambling down the littered sidewalk. The lights from a dozen motels flashed on and off. Through the windows of an all-night Laundromat he could see a lone woman folding clothes on a bare table.

"Welcome—to—Holly-wood," Travis crooned into the windshield. "Where the . . ." he began. "No. Where you're . . ." Travis started again with a slightly different melody. He frowned and stopped.

"Why do I keep thinking I'm such a hot songwriter?" he said wearily, stepping on the gas to pass the slow-moving white Cadillac in front of him. "Let's face it, Travis Bennett. You are a limo driver. That's all. A driver who wants to be a musician. But you're not. And you may never be."

Travis bent his mouth into a sad smile. "And on top of everything else, Winnie is gone. Married. Out of my life, probably forever," he said softly. "Thanks a lot, Liza Ruff, for ruining my life. I mean, couldn't you have broken it to me gently, instead of blurting it out as if it didn't matter?"

Clenching his fist on the steering wheel, Travis pressed down the accelerator. He'd been thinking about Winnie nonstop since the day before yesterday, when Liza had unceremoniously dumped the news on him. Winnie had even called the night before, claiming to have important news for Liza.

But he never did tell Liza or call Winnie back. It was too painful.

After all, Winnie had been his first real love. Their time in Europe the summer before had been an incredible fantasy. But now he realized his feelings for her had been more serious than that. He cared about her deeply.

Travis glanced dully out the window as the BMWs, Jaguars, and Mercedes began the daylong traffic jam as they approached Rodeo Drive. Through all the tough times he'd been having, it had been the thought of Winnie that had kept him going. Smart, warm, quirky Winnie. Now she was gone.

His shoulder-length hair whipping against the muggy air, Travis took a deep breath and let it out slowly.

Then there was Liza. The image of her stranded on Sunset Boulevard waiting for him made him feel guiltier by the second. He knew he'd promised to pick her up after her big meeting with Bernie Greenberg. But he'd been too upset about Winnie to deal with her.

Travis smiled a little. "If anyone could scam her way out of a situation, it's Liza. She probably talked Greenberg himself into driving her to the motel." He remembered the hungry, excited look on her face when she came off the plane. He shook his head. He didn't even have the heart to tell her that he was only a lowly limo driver, not a big-shot musician. It didn't seem right to shove reality right in her face the moment she arrived in Hollywood. Everyone deserved to have their little fantasy. At least for a day or so.

Travis chuckled to himself. Liza reminded him of his own first day in L.A. several months ago, when he buzzed in on his motorcycle, fresh from his reunion with Winnie on the U. of S. campus.

He'd been on top of the world. Then, after the dog-eat-dog reality of the place had sunk in, he'd been determined. Then, after too many canceled gigs and empty promises from the recording studios, he'd gotten angry. Then desperate. Then he'd gotten this job.

Travis swung the limo into the swank front driveway of the Beverly Hills Hotel and hopped out of his car. There was something voluptuous and cartoon-like about the hotel's pink paint job and shaggy palm trees. Inside, dozens of hip-looking L.A. types were casually hanging out, talking on their cellular phones, and checking themselves in mirrors.

He could almost picture Liza here, right at home, sauntering proudly down past the pink flowerpots toward the shimmering pool, a tight 1940s swimsuit hugging her generous body.

"White Line Limos?" the bellhop was saying loudly.

Travis looked over. "Oh . . . oh, yeah. Sorry. Where are the bags?"

After slipping the suitcases in the trunk, Travis opened the back door politely and let the two businessmen in. His mind was still on Winnie. And his conscience was still on Liza.

The drive back from the airport was slow and unnerving. Traffic was backed up on the freeway, the smog was thick, and a few harassed drivers were darting dangerously around the limo, desperately trying to get ahead.

L.A. was a tough town. Travis couldn't stop thinking about what it might do to Liza. Was she okay? How *was* she getting around? He knew she didn't have much money and taxies were expensive.

Was Liza actually having her screen tests and power lunches? Or was she broke and discouraged and desperate like every other Hollywood hopeful he'd ever met?

Suddenly, Travis flicked on his turn signal and nudged his way off the freeway toward Sunset Boulevard. He had to at least find out. Liza seemed like a good kid. He had no right to desert her in this crazy city, just because Winnie Gottlieb had gotten married.

It doesn't have anything to do with Liza. It's about me and Winnie, he decided. That's all.

By the time he finally arrived at the Tropicana Motel's entrance, the morning smog had thickened and L.A. seemed like a steamy sea of soup a person could get lost in—or drown.

Almost immediately he found Liza by the pool's edge, dipping her white legs into the water and staring glumly into space. Behind her were the first-floor rooms of the courtyard motel, and a group of funky plastic flamingos was stuck near the base of a decorative palm tree. "Hi." Travis stopped behind her.

Liza jumped and put a hand to her chest. "*What?* Oh god. Don't scare me like that. I haven't talked to anyone important in forty-eight hours."

"Sorry," Travis said quietly, slipping his hands into his pockets and wondering if Liza really was someone he could relate to, or whether she was just another crazy person trying to claw her way up the Hollywood ladder. It wasn't always easy to tell.

For a moment Travis thought Liza was going to break out into a grateful smile. But then her red lips hardened. "Hey, thanks for the ride you promised.

Let me tell you. My feet really appreciated it."

"Liza, there's something I—"

"What could you possibly tell me?" Liza interrupted. She lifted her hot-pink toes out of the water and talked to them. "Go on, thank Mr. Bennett for that invigorating four-mile walk in Liza's spiked heels. Go on, tell him how it was a real character-building experience. Show him your blisters, okay?"

Travis sat gloomily at the edge of a lounge chair near her. His eyes traveled curiously over her outfit, which consisted of a tight, green halter top covered with pictures of brightly colored fruit, and a short, swingy white skirt. Her orange-red hair had been tied back with a band that matched her top. A pair of strapless, high-heeled sandals lay next to the pool. "I came to say I was sorry, Liza."

"Oh, well, I'll tell you, that does me a lot of good," Liza snapped back, staring down at her toenails.

Travis bristled. For a moment, he was tempted to leave. Was she just another neurotic actress who thought the world would lie down at her feet the moment she hit Hollywood?

"Listen," Liza slowed, "I've had a bad couple of days, okay? The damn producer stalled me. I never did get the big screen test and audition he hyped in his letter. In fact, I won't get to see him until tomorrow morning at ten."

"Well, then I'm sorry about that, too," Travis murmured. "Liza . . . this town can be really tough. Even if you do have great connections and everything."

"Tell me about it."

"Listen," Travis began awkwardly, "I haven't been honest with you about a couple of things."

Travis watched as Liza turned her head around and pulled one shapely leg up onto the side of the pool. Her blue eyes seemed to light up, as if she were the sort of person who enjoyed secrets. Or confessions. Then her lips slowly spread into a giant smile that showed off her straight, white teeth. "So. Spill. What's the big mystery?"

"It's about Winnie." Travis clasped his hands together and stared down at his feet. "I guess she didn't tell you much about our relationship."

Liza's mouth dropped open. "She said you were an old friend."

"Yeah, well, it was more than that—to me, at least," Travis struggled. "We'd spent a lot of time in Europe together last summer. So when you told me that she'd married Josh Gaffey, it was just really bad news for me."

"Ahhhhhhh," Liza replied, placing a finger thoughtfully on her chin.

"I took it out on you, Liza," Travis admitted. "I just didn't want to think about Winnie or any of her friends ever again. I'm sorry."

"That's okay," Liza said lightly. "Gee. Winnie

never really told me about you." She paused, thinking. " Oh, well, L.A.'s loaded with beautiful girls who want to pair off with hunky musician-types like you, darling. You'll get over it."

"That's the other thing, Liza."

"There's more? Hey, this is getting interesting." Liza drew her other foot out of the water and hugged her knees with excitement. Travis stared at her bright red hair, which swept down over her pale shoulders. Sure, she was kind of unconventional-looking, but he liked her smooth skin and offbeat, corny beauty. He was starting to like her.

"I'm not really a big-shot musician." Travis looked her straight in the eye. "At least, not yet. I actually haven't had much luck. That big car I was driving wasn't mine either. It belongs to the limousine company I work for."

"Oh," Liza whispered. "Is that why you're wearing that funny white shirt?

"Sorry." Travis dropped his head. "You should see my funny hat, too. It's in the car."

Liza giggled. "I'd love to see it."

Travis looked up slowly and saw that she was staring at him with shining eyes. She didn't seem to care that he wasn't a hot musician. She looked almost relieved. "Look, let me make it up to you. I'll drive you to and from your appointment tomorrow. And I'll give you the full limo treatment."

Liza's eyes sparkled. "It's a deal," she said, slipping her feet back in the water. "Maybe it will help. You wouldn't believe how many people I've met down here at the pool in the last couple of days. Dozens of people just like me who've spent their last dime getting out here. And all they usually get is a slap in the face. Or some kind of weirdo come-on."

"I believe it." Travis slid down so that he was lying on his stomach next to her, trailing his hand in the water. "This town jerks people around, but it's some kind of magnet for dreamers. One in a million hits the jackpot. Most everyone else is lucky if they get out of town before they end up in the streets."

"Yeah." Liza nodded. "I hear you."

"The people who do stick around . . . like me, for instance," Travis continued, "none of us are what we do. The limo drivers are really songwriters. The waitresses are really actresses. The bellhops are really writers. It seems like everyone you meet has come from somewhere else. Everyone's here with a dream."

Liza looked at him over her shoulder and wiggled her toes. "So far, it sounds pretty good. Hey, my parents sold office furniture in Brooklyn. I'd rather starve in paradise than get fat in the abyss."

Travis laughed.

"Hey." Liza lifted her feet out of the pool and turned to face him. "Don't feel bad about not having a Grammy yet. You've only been here a few months."

"I'm making progress, though," Travis said casually, propping his head up on one elbow and looking over at her. "That's the thing about poverty and solitude. It makes you hungry. I've written more than a dozen new songs in the last three months."

"Really?" Liza squeaked. "Will you sing one for me?"

"Sure," Travis said, grinning at her. She seemed so eager and carefree. She almost made him feel the excitement of arriving in L.A. all over again. "The main thing is that I have the songs and I've put together the bucks to have a bunch of demo tapes made. Now I spend all my free time dropping them off at the record companies."

"Wow."

Travis shrugged. "Or at the offices of the guys who manage the recording artists. They're always looking for the right song their dude can sing. Hey, it's one way to see all the glitzed-out receptionists in this town. They all thank me very much and smile."

"Cheer up," Liza said, reaching out and patting Travis on the leg. "Someone'll give you a call pretty soon. You'll get your break. We both will."

Travis looked at Liza's face. She was so open and unrehearsed, he felt himself relaxing for the first time in a long while. For a brief moment, their eyes locked. Then a door slammed somewhere. A woman wearing a skintight dress and a long blond wig walked past them and glanced approvingly at Travis.

"I'll let you in on a secret," he whispered.

"Ooo, what?"

"Be cool."

"I already *am* cool." Liza giggled, planting her hand on her hip. "Can't you see?"

"No," Travis said, serious. "What I mean is, you've got to keep your spirits up. Be cool even when you're feeling lousy. In Hollywood, they smell desperation on you like blood."

Liza lifted a knee up and posed. "Act as if I have a hundred other offers waiting in the wings."

Travis nodded. "You got it. Remember my big act when I picked you up at the airport?"

"Oh, yeah," Liza drawled, "Mr. Big Shot."

"You assumed I was a big, successful recording artist. You assumed the fancy car was mine," Travis explained.

"Sure. You looked like you owned the place."

"See? It's my new attitude. The come-and-get-me-not-that-I-really-need-you look. Since I tried it on, I'm actually getting past those receptionists once in a while. People are starting to listen to my tapes."

"Something's going to break." Liza held her hand out and Travis slapped it down playfully. "I can feel it in my hot blood."

"Yow!" Travis grinned at her. Suddenly, they were just sitting there, staring at each other. A maid slowly rolled a cart full of cleaning supplies past them. A thread of hope slipped through him. Had he actually found someone he could talk to in this crazy place?

"Well?"

"Well." Travis stood up. "If we're so hot, then we'll have to paint the town. Tomorrow night."

"I'm broke," Liza said, shrugging.

"No. I want to show you *my* L.A. The Venice pier. Foot-long hot dogs at the beach. Hanging out at the International House of Pancakes."

For a moment Liza hesitated. "Well, I don't think Rich would mind," she said quickly. "In fact he's not really a boyfriend or anything. I mean, I've only gone out with him a couple of times."

"Liza," Travis said quietly. "I'll pick you up at six o'clock. Right after you've landed the lead in that new TV series. You're going to love this place. I can tell you're going to love it just like I do."

# Eleven

..................................................

"**B**rucie Botka! Time out!" A haggard-looking young woman was screeching from a bench near Winnie at the edge of the neighborhood playground.

Winnie's head jerked up from her Western Civ study notes. The morning sun was streaming through the ancient elms and a distant lawn mower hummed in the background. When she first arrived an hour earlier at the off-campus park, she'd hoped to calm herself with pleasant scenes of happy parents playing with their chubby-faced toddlers.

In a couple of hours, she'd be taking her colossal

Western Civ exam. It was important for her to be in the right frame of mind.

But so far she had a weird feeling the early-morning play slot had been reserved exclusively for the nation's future warriors and illegal junk bond traders.

"Brucie!" The woman called out again, her huge denim jumper flapping as she stalked across the sand, a second, smaller child dangling from her hip. Her hair looked as if it had once been in a braid, but had been clawed apart by small birds. "GET OVER HERE NOW!"

Winnie followed her with her eyes, nervously flipping the corner of her notes with a perfect, coral-pink fingernail.

"He's eighteen months," the woman said, flopping down next to Winnie. "And you know what they say." She slid the baby down on her lap.

Winnie cleared her throat. "Um . . . no. What do they say?"

The woman turned and looked at Winnie curiously. "You know. Things are great when they're one. Lousy at eighteen months. Great at two . . ."

"Lousy at two-and-a-half," Winnie completed her sentence, feeling slightly ill. She felt weird in her neon polka dot jogging shorts and matching lime-green tank top.

"Yeah! You read that, too," the woman said, relieved. "So. Which one's yours?"

Winnie suddenly felt like a spy. "Um. I'm here alone. I'm studying for a test."

"Oh."

"I . . . I'm a student at the U. of S.," Winnie tried to explain, but she knew it didn't make sense. Quickly, she glanced at the baby on the woman's lap. It sort of looked like a girl, Winnie thought. She tilted her head to the side and frowned at the grubby knees on its terry cloth sleeper. The child suddenly lifted her eyes, fixed on Winnie, and abruptly burst into tears.

"Ah!" Winnie jumped up.

"Aw, come on, darling," the woman cooed wearily. She turned and gave Winnie a knowing look. "Up all night with the teething."

"Oh, how terrible."

Winnie realized that the woman was giving her a strange look, as if she'd suddenly decided Winnie didn't belong in the playground with her children.

*Of course I don't belong here,* Winnie thought desperately. *I only just graduated from the playground myself. I'm still a kid. Look at me. Not a wrinkle in sight. Not a sign of maturity within two miles. I still eat Cap'n Crunch cereal for breakfast and sometimes forget to brush between meals. How am I supposed to tell a child what to do when I don't even know myself?*

"Bye," Winnie whispered, stuffing her study notes into the pages of her Western Civ text and heading across the park's large lawn, toward home. Her eyes were puffy from studying since five in the morning. But she hadn't been able to sleep.

If only she could talk to Josh. If only Faith would call her back.

*Where was Faith? Couldn't she tell Winnie was having a crisis? No. All Faith could do was study and hang out with her weird new roommate. It was a nightmare.*

When Winnie finally trudged up the steps of her small off-campus bungalow, Josh's bike was already gone from the porch. Thumping her purse down on the shiny hardwood floor in the entryway, she immediately headed for the living room, shoved a CD into the disc player, and turned the volume up.

*Maybe I could take the baby to class with me in one of those slings,* Winnie thought as she sank down at the kitchen table and tried to picture herself with a baby. *And then we'd go to the playground at night after I'd finished studying for all my classes. Josh could put the baby in the bassinet or something while he's working at the computer. . . .*

The loud music suddenly softened and one of Winnie and Josh's roommates, Rich Greenberg, walked in, frowning. "I like B-Bruce Springsteen, Win. B-but not at eight A.M."

Winnie's eyes flashed up. When she saw Rich, all she could think of was Liza. She could hardly believe that he'd actually forged a letter from his Hollywood producer dad—and had conned Liza into going to L.A. Poor Liza!

"You are not a very nice person, Rich," Winnie burst out. "Do you know that?"

"Huh?" Rich rubbed his eyes sleepily and opened the refrigerator door.

Winnie crossed her arms across her chest and tipped her chair back. "Josh and I found the forged letter you sent to Liza," she challenged. "How could you do it? Liza thinks your father actually wrote to her and she's down in Los Angeles right now, about to be totally humiliated."

For a few moments it looked as if Rich had been momentarily paralyzed. Winnie continued to stare coldly at him until the fridge began humming loudly and Rich calmly closed the door.

"So." Rich turned around with a strange, victorious look on his face. "Now you know."

"Yeah." Winnie picked up an orange from the fruit bowl and threw it at him. It hit him on the shoulder. "And we hope Liza knows, too. We tried to contact her last night through my friend Travis. What you've done is heartless, Rich. Liza shouldn't have stolen your dummy, but she didn't deserve this cruelty."

"Liza's sick and you know it," Rich replied with a steady, quiet growl that sent a shiver up Winnie's spine. "She ruined my one chance to make something of myself. I would have won that contest, Winnie."

"Maybe you would and maybe you wouldn't have," Winnie cried out. "But your plot to get back at Liza makes me ill. Sure, she made a mistake. A lousy mistake but a *human* mistake made in a moment of anger. Your move was something totally different, Rich."

"People do what they have to do," Rich replied, turning on his heel as Winnie collapsed her head into her arms in frustration. "Rich!" she yelled. "Did Faith call me back this morning?"

"No," she could hear him yelling down the hall before the door to his room slammed and the house was completely silent again.

Winnie could never bear to be surrounded by silence. Loud music, arguing, laughing, crackling junk food wrappers, anything. Anything but silence.

She'd never felt so alone. Yesterday, she'd tried to get Josh to have lunch with her at the Beanery, but he had a million excuses. A computer program due. An exam. A paper. Last night he'd left for the library as soon as the word *baby* slipped from her lips. He hadn't really talked with her since they'd found out about the pregnancy the week before.

Then Faith had deserted her. And her other best friend, KC Angeletti, had practically disappeared from sight with her new boyfriend, Cody Wainwright.

"I can't do this," Winnie blurted to herself, leaping up from the table. She was sick. She was lonely. She was facing the biggest predicament of her whole life. She thought being married was hard. Being married *and* pregnant was about as easy as running blindfolded through an obstacle course designed by Spanish inquisition torture experts.

Winnie slipped quietly down the hall, opened the door to her room, and slumped down in the chair that faced her old-fashioned vanity and mirror.

"Hello, Winnie Gottlieb," she whispered. Though the room behind her reflection was cluttered with clothes, computer disks, books and clumps of towels, it was completely quiet, as if a tornado had just blown through. She stared at the pale, expressionless face staring back at her in the mirror.

"What are you doing?" Winnie asked herself, biting back tears. "May I ask you what you are doing? You've got to get out of this slump."

Winnie brightened her expression and fluffed her spiky hair up a little. Then she took a tube of hot-pink lipstick off the dresser and applied it liberally to her lips. "What do you mean?" she replied, cheerfully shocked. "I am attending a fine university that, by the way, is rather difficult to get into. I am about to ace an important history exam. I am married to a wonderful guy and have many, many friends. And if that weren't enough, I volunteer many hours each week at the Crisis Hotline, helping those who are less fortunate than myself. Any other questions?"

Winnie yanked the last tissue out of a box and blotted the lipstick. Then she scowled at the mirror. "You are so full of bull," she declared. "Your life, in fact, is down the tubes. You got married too early, thinking it was going to be just another lark. Then you managed to forget your birth control one fine afternoon and got yourself pregnant. You are a teenage pregnancy statistic, Winnie. Ignored by your husband. And deserted by your friends."

Tears began to spill out of Winnie's eyes. She screwed her face into a crazy grin. "That's just not so," she wept. "Your life will go on. You'll have a beautiful baby. You and Josh will work it out. You'll both graduate from college with honors and go on to wonderful jobs doing the work you love. You'll look back on this and wonder why you worried about it so much."

She sighed. "How are you going to stay in school?" she asked her reflection.

*Josh and I will work it out.*

"It will never work out. Go home and stay with your mother. She'll help you with the baby."

*But I can't live without Josh!*

Winnie suddenly stood up, turned around, and flung herself down on the bed, sobbing. She dragged herself up on the disheveled bed and tried to think.

What had happened? She and Josh had been so together. So in sync. Winnie wanted to be that way again. She had to get Josh's attention somehow!

Spying a pack of Post-It notes on Josh's desk, she got up, grabbed a pen, and began scribbling.

*Josh*, she wrote. *I love you. Please talk to me.* Winnie ripped the note off the top and stuck it on Josh's computer screen.

*Josh, I need you desperately*, she wrote on another note. She ran out into the kitchen, opened the freezer, and stuck the note on a carton of Josh's favorite ice cream.

*Josh, I'm leaving you.* Winnie lifted the telephone receiver, stuck the note on it, and slammed it down. Her hands shaking, Winnie jerked open a kitchen drawer and pulled out a bus schedule.

*Josh, If I'm not here, I've left on the one o'clock bus for Jacksonville. Good-bye.* Winnie ran down the hall and stuck the message on the toilet seat.

For a moment, Winnie stared at her words. Then she realized it all made sense. Josh needed to be shocked into facing the facts. After her exam, she'd pack her things, and find Faith. Then she'd just blurt out the news about the baby. Faith would pay attention to her then. It didn't have to be the right moment. She'd just blurt it out and make Faith realize that her situation was serious.

After that, there was no way Faith wouldn't help. "I'll tell her I'm going back home to stay with my mom and make her take me to the bus station,"

Winnie said firmly. "When Josh finds my notes, he'll rush downtown, see that Faith is about to take over the problem, and whisk me back home. He'll apologize. And then we'll be okay."

Winnie knew she had the right plan. All she had to do was find Faith and spill the news. After that, she knew, Faith would do exactly what she told her to do.

# Twelve

·····················

aith woke up, yawned, and smiled happily to herself. Her eye still shut, she pulled the sheets up around her chin, amazed that she was actually savoring the thought of taking an exam.

Even though Brooks had selfishly kept her up until midnight, Becker's last-minute effort to save her really worked. For once, she was completely prepared. For once, she was rested and optimistic. Her brain was already beginning to tally off dozens of important dates, the names of key Renaissance figures. Her mind was clicking with Becker's incredible, logical advice on how to attack Professor Hermann's likely essay questions.

By ten o'clock she'd be ready to knock Professor Hermann's socks off.

Faith opened her eyes. The room was quiet and still. Her heartbeat quickened slightly. Then she sat up and looked around the room nervously. Something was wrong. Becker had left early for his eight o'clock class. That wasn't unusual. What was it? She listened for the usual bustling, banging sounds in the hall, of students racing into the bathroom or off to class.

But there was only silence.

The light in the room was flat and bright.

Faith sat up like a shot and grabbed the clock off her desk.

*Ten-thirty-three.*

At first, Faith just stared at it. Then, slowly, her mind began to kick in. She couldn't breathe. Her muscles refused to work.

*"The exam,"* Faith cried out, jumping out of bed. *"I've missed the exam!"* Suddenly, her stomach felt like she'd swallowed a brick. Still clutching the clock, she lifted it up, horrified, checked it again, then threw it into the corner of the room.

*BZZZZZZZZZZZZZZZZZZZZZZZZZZZZZZZZ*, the alarm began buzzing crazily. Tears flooding her eyes, Faith ducked down, grabbed the clock, and turned it off. "Why couldn't you have done that two and a half hours ago?" She moaned, sinking down into a heap on the floor. "Why did you have to pick this day to break? Why did Brooks have to keep me out so late? Why is everything turning out this way?"

Curling her knees up to her chin, all Faith could do for a while was weep. When she first arrived at U. of S. she knew that things could be tough in one's freshman year. She knew there'd be a lot of pressure and competition. But nothing had prepared her for this. It wasn't just the intensity in her own life. It was the craziness in everyone else's life that kept creeping up behind her. Sabotaging her.

After a few minutes Faith heard the sound of jangling keys and the door slowly opening. She looked up. It was Becker. Wearing a black T-shirt, a pair of form-fitting blue jeans, and his shiny hair in a pony-tail, he was the usual picture of calm, deliberate movement.

He stared hard at her.

"I blew it," Faith said softly, looking at him, then dropping her chin. Her loose hair spilled over her shoulders.

"I don't understand," Becker said quietly, his pale blue eyes widening with concern. "Why are you here? The exam . . ."

Faith reached for the broken clock. "This," she said, her voice cracking, her mind whiting out, "did not go off." She drew her hands up to her face and sobbed.

Becker looked at her sadly, dropped his book bag,

and sat down next to her. Slowly, his hand slipped around her shoulders and down her back. He stroked her back with his strong, sure hand. "I'm really sorry."

"I know," Faith squeaked, still looking down, ashamed. "I know."

"I feel terrible." Becker let his hand fall. "I could have woken you up before I left for my eight o'clock—"

"I know," Faith interrupted.

"If I'd only known your clock wasn't reliable."

"It's not just my clock," Faith burst out suddenly, lifting her head. Her eyes felt like they were on fire. "It's my *life* that's unreliable. *People* who are unreliable."

"Yeah," Becker murmured sympathetically.

Faith trembled. "I'm sorry."

"I know."

"I'm scared, Becker," Faith said. "I'm scared. I'm not used to this feeling."

"You have to face it, Faith. Your friends take advantage of you," Becker said carefully.

"It's not their fault!" Faith cried out. "It's mine. I don't tell them what I need."

Becker shook his head and stood up. "Listen to me, Faith. I'm going to help you, and believe me, I'm the only one who is here for you right now."

Faith stared up at him.

"The first thing I want you to do is take a shower.

While you're doing that I'll go down to the dining commons and bring something up for you to eat."

"Okay," Faith said meekly.

"Then you can get yourself together, get over to Professor Hermann's office by eleven-thirty and arrange a makeup exam." Becker strode over to his book bag and pulled out his calendar.

"Okay," Faith answered, not knowing what else to say.

Becker ran a finger down a page of his calendar. "I'll go over to the library right now and scour the stacks for anything that might help you with the *Taming of the Shrew* presentation. We have until tomorrow afternoon."

"Gee," Faith said, her eyes filling with weary but grateful tears. The burst of energy and euphoria she'd awakened with had now vanished completely. "I'd really appreciate it, Becker. My mind's more of a blank than ever."

"I have a seminar all afternoon," Becker said hurriedly, "but I'll meet you back here at eight o'clock tonight, we'll go over the *Shrew* material I've dug up, and we'll get you into that program."

Suddenly Becker's call to action was making Faith a little dizzy. It was as if every possible pressure were converging on her at once, overwhelming her. She just didn't have the strength to fight it. All of a sudden, she wanted nothing more than to curl up in her bed and forget everything. Faith pressed the edge of her trembling hand to her forehead. "I can't do this . . ."

"Yes, you can."

"No," Faith mumbled. "I'm not like you, Becker. I'm not driven enough. I can't do it anymore."

Faith could feel Becker sit down quietly next to her on the bed. She could smell the clean scent of his soft shirt. He reached his hand under her hair and gently massaged her neck, sending waves of tingly warmth down her back. "Yes, you can. You have more power than you think."

Faith breathed in deeply, feeling his expert fingers at the back of her head. She flopped it forward, relaxing. "You make it sound so easy," she breathed.

"It is," Becker said, reaching over with his other hand and lifting her chin up. He smiled, then he bent his head down and gently pressed his lips to hers.

At first Faith felt a sensation in her lips. Then it spread through her entire body. Never before had such a gentle kiss given her such a powerful feeling. She felt so loved. So cared for. She opened her eyes and looked into his. She took in his shiny dark hair, his quietly handsome face and cleft chin. Then she kissed him back, slipping her arms up around his back.

When they drew apart, Faith's heart was pounding. "This isn't supposed to be happening."

"Why, Faith?" Becker's eyes were pleading.

"Because . . . this is an experiment in living between men and women . . ." Faith stumbled, staring helplessly at him, "who aren't, you know, *involved*. We're supposed to be just friends, remember?"

Becker smiled at her tenderly, then leaned his head back against the wall, still stroking her back lightly with the flat of his hand. "Yes, but . . . do you really want another friend right now, Faith?"

Faith could feel a smile slipping onto her face. She knew what he meant. "Well . . ."

"Maybe what you need is someone who is more than a friend," Becker said softly, getting up and reaching for his book bag. "Someone who truly cares about you. Like I do."

Faith's mouth dropped open. But she returned Becker's steady gaze as he opened the door, then disappeared into the hall.

A half-hour later Faith was racing past Plotsky Fountain. When she entered the building's crowded hallway she realized that the entire Western Civ class had just finished the exam and was headed tiredly out of the amphitheater.

Faith ducked her head into the dusty room. Its semicircular rows of desks pointed down toward Professor Hermann's podium, where he stood, shuffling through a fresh stack of exam papers. Down by the classroom's side entrance she spotted KC, Lauren, and Winnie whispering together.

Taking a deep breath, Faith marched down the steps toward the front of the room. "Um . . . Excuse me. Professor Hermann?"

Professor Hermann took off his bifocals and leaned forward on the podium so that he was looking down at her.

Faith screwed up her courage. "Professor Hermann. I'm Faith Crowley. I'm in this class. And . . . um, I'm afraid I missed the exam. I'm wondering if I could take a makeup test."

Professor Hermann sighed and stared out over his beaklike nose. "Yes, yes, yes," he said impatiently. "Don't even tell me what happened. I can't stand to hear another excuse. Your grandmother died. You were locked in your room. You slept in."

Faith looked down sheepishly. She felt like a guilty little girl returning a stick of candy she'd stolen from the drugstore. "I'm terribly sorry . . ."

"You have one chance to make this up," Professor Hermann said tersely. "Be here at five o'clock sharp this afternoon."

"But—" Faith began. She had hoped to take the test immediately, so she could spend the rest of the day on her drama presentation. But she stopped in midsentence when she saw her professor's annoyed look. She dropped her eyes. "Thank you very much. I'll be here."

"Fine."

*"Faith!"* She heard Lauren's voice behind her.

Faith abruptly turned around. Lauren and Winnie were both stomping down the stairs in her direction, as KC slipped quietly out the side door.

"Hi," Faith said simply, walking wearily toward them.

*"Faith!"* Lauren practically yelled. "I've been trying to reach you for *days.*"

Faith felt a flush of rising impatience, but managed to control it. "I'm sorry, Lauren. It's been a really bad week for me. Let's get together this weekend when I've recovered."

Lauren scowled at her, and Faith could see Winnie thumping down the stairs behind her, pale and weary. "You haven't had *one minut*e to pick up the phone and answer my call?" Lauren demanded. Her hair was sticking out all over her head and her violet eyes were flashing like a warning beacon. "I absolutely have to talk with you right away!"

"Okay!" Faith practically shouted, stepping around her on the stairs and heading angrily toward the exit. "I'll get back to you when I can, Lauren."

Faith felt a hand grip her arm as Lauren stormed off. *"We have to talk. I need you desperately!"*

Faith looked back at Winnie and felt her heart drop a little. She'd never seen her close friend look so haggard. Her large brown eyes had dark circles under them, and it looked as if she hadn't even bothered to put on any makeup except for a wide smear of red lipstick. Even her usually spiky hair looked droopy. "Winnie?" Faith asked. "What's wrong?"

"Please, Faith," Winnie breathed desperately. "I've *got* to talk to you."

"But Winnie . . ."

*"Why didn't you call me back . . . ?"* Winnie wailed softly, clutching her notebook as if she were drowning at sea.

Faith's eyes darted instinctively around the room, which was now completely empty. "Win. What's going on?"

Winnie started to sob openly. "Please," she gasped, taking Faith's arm and gripping it. "Please, Faith. If you've ever cared anything about me, help me now."

Faith tried to think. Winnie had always been a little dramatic when she had problems. In fact, Faith couldn't remember the number of times Winnie had blown things out of proportion in high school, and gotten everyone totally worried over the simplest thing. In a way, Faith had become hardened to it. And yet . . .

"Faith, *please*." Winnie grabbed Faith's shoulder. "I'm facing the biggest crisis of my life and I need someone."

Faith looked at her, defeated. "But I've got a makeup test in just a few hours. And I'm totally unprepared for the Professional Theater Program presentation tomorrow, Win. It's so important to me."

Winnie's eyes were pleading with her. "It's a matter of life and death, Faith. And I need you to go with me to the bus station right now."

"Life and death?" Faith whispered. Winnie had never gone that far in high school. "Is there something wrong with Josh?"

Winnie tightened her grip on Faith's arm and began dragging her up the stairs. "If you'd let me talk to you in private, I can explain," Winnie pleaded.

"You're scaring me, Win. Stop it."

"I'm not exaggerating, Faith," Winnie insisted. The door slammed behind them and the two of them were suddenly alone in the ancient building's musty-smelling main hallway. Faith followed Winnie's skintight polka dot shorts to the bottom step of the main staircase, sat down, and took a deep breath. She was tired and her head hurt.

"Okay," Faith finally said. "What's wrong?"

"I'm pregnant."

Faith's mouth dropped open. All of a sudden she couldn't breathe or think. "What?"

Winnie sucked in her breath. "God it feels good to tell you this, Faith. I've been keeping it for so long—" Winnie broke off, crying.

"Oh, Win," Faith grabbed Winnie and hugged her hard. "Oh my god, Win. What does Josh say?"

"He . . . he isn't dealing with it, Faith," Winnie sobbed. "He won't talk. We've known for a couple of weeks and he's acting like it happened to his second cousin once removed in Lincoln, Nebraska—not to us."

"I can't believe it," Faith breathed. "Josh Gaffey is one of the most loving, patient, wonderful guys I've ever met."

"So," Winnie began bravely. "I'm going to go to my mom's for a while. Maybe that will shake him up. I've got to do something and you have to help me. You're the only one who can."

Suddenly flooded with conviction and love, Faith stood up and took Winnie's hand. "When does your bus leave?"

"In an hour and a half." Winnie cried softly. "I'm going home to grab a few things. Then I'm going to walk downtown. And I need you to come with me."

"Don't you worry, Win. I'm going to be right there, by your side," Faith said calmly. In her mind she knew Becker was right. Today was critical to her grades, and maybe even to her future in the theater. It was no time to be distracted. But in her heart all Faith knew was that Winnie needed her. And there was no way she was going to let her down.

# *Thirteen*

. . . . . . . . . . . . . . . . . . . . . . . . . . . . . . . . . . . .

"**I** still can't believe I'm wearing this," Liza
was chattering as she slid into the soft
leather front seat next to Travis.

With only half an hour to go before her interview with television mogul Bernie Greenberg, Liza
felt as if she were about to jump off a cliff. The
only trouble was, she didn't know if she would be
soaring on wings of gold, or plummeting to the
rocks below.

Travis stepped on the accelerator and pulled past the
Tropicana Motel's neon palm-tree sign. "Hey, I can't
believe what I'm wearing, either," he said, grinning.

Liza couldn't help laughing, too. Travis was wearing his official limo driver's uniform, a white, short-sleeved shirt and a dark hat with a brim. "But look at me." Liza glanced down at her plain black stirrup pants, short black boots, and sleeveless white blouse, shuddering. "I wore my only decent outfit to the *last* interview, which turned out to be a bust. And now I can't wear it again because I'd look like a loser."

"But you're wearing what actresses usually wear to auditions," Travis explained, running an eye down her body, then turning onto Sunset Boulevard. "Especially the busy ones."

Liza looked at Travis as if he were crazy. "Are you kidding? This outfit is a zero. *Nada* personality. I look like a prison inmate. A boarder in a religious convent. The sample lady at the supermarket—"

"Liza," Travis interrupted, a smile slipping out of the corner of his mouth. Liza's eyes took in the deep line creasing the side of his tanned face. His tiny gold earring peeking out from his shoulder-length hair. "We've been over this before, man. Black and white. It's cool. It's hip. It tells people that you look beyond clothing for your image."

"Okay. Okay." Liza nodded.

"You've got to make Bernie Greenberg believe that you have other gigs going. Other people to see. Options. Don't look desperate or he'll think he's looking at rejected material."

"Right."

"Besides, you look good." Travis nodded with approval.

Liza lifted one shoulder in a modest shrug and smiled back. She patted her hair. Travis always made her feel so normal. It didn't matter that she goofed up, said strange things, and probably made way too much noise for the ordinary jerks of the world. Travis was different. He just kind of sat back and took her in. She didn't have the urge to entertain him, or smother him—like she did with Rich, for instance.

"Want me to go in with you?" Travis offered, finally pulling into the building's parking lot and setting the brake. "Hey, I bet I could get a buzz just sitting in Greenberg's office picking up on the high anxiety levels."

Liza giggled. "Sure. Why not?"

*"Nee nee nee nee,"* Travis sang through his teeth. *"Nee nee nee nee."* He tucked his chin down to his chest and deepened his voice. *"Meet Liza Ruff. A beautiful young actress on her way to her first big audition in sunny Los Angeles. What she doesn't know is that she is about to experience alien beings disguised as Hollywood producers and the actors they control. What she doesn't know is— that she is about to enter . . . the Twilight Zone."*

Liza was still laughing at Travis when the elevator in Bernie Greenberg's office building swooshed open. *"Shh!"* she hissed, giggling.

But when she pushed open the glass doors and

headed into the elegant reception area again, her anxiety returned and her pulse immediately soared into the ozone layer. "Hello." Liza faked a bright smile. "I'm Liza Ruff returning to see Mr. Greenberg."

"Oh, right." The same hip receptionist smiled. "Please have a seat, Liza. He'll be right with you."

Sitting down carefully next to Travis, Liza could practically hear her blood throbbing in her head. Her palms were too sweaty to pick up a magazine and she felt about ten times uglier, fatter, and dumber than anyone who had ever walked through these doors.

"Miss Ruff?" A woman with long, blond hair and a trim knit suit stuck her head out of the door to Mr. Greenberg's inner office.

Liza stood up dizzily and wiggled her fingers back at Travis. "Wish me luck."

"You're hot," he whispered, clenching his fist and raising it slightly.

Liza followed the blond woman into a large, carpeted office, dominated by a sleek desk and a metal sculpture in the corner of the room. Two leather couches faced each other, joined by a third one, which faced the desk.

Behind the desk, a burly man with dark curly hair was talking and laughing loudly into the telephone. Liza's mouth fell open. Despite the luxurious office, Bernie himself was dressed in a rumpled tennis outfit. "Please have a seat here," the woman murmured, pointing to one of the couches. "Bernie won't be long."

"Yeah, yeah, yeah, Max," Bernie was bellowing good-naturedly into the receiver. "That's what Bobby always says. And he never means it. He wants to do it. He needs the dough. And he's holding out on us for more. Trust me on this."

Liza felt a thrill zip up her spine. Here she was in the Hollywood office of a big producer. She was dying. Who was Bobby? She squinted her eyes and stared at Bernie Greenberg's round face and balding head. He was very tan and didn't look anything like Rich.

"Yeah. Yeah. Fine. Good. No. Yes. Okay. That's what I said. Okay." Liza watched, fascinated, as Bernie gave a final laugh and slammed the phone down enthusiastically. Then he looked up at her.

Liza stared back, terrified.

"So," Bernie said with a sigh. His pudgy face broke into a grin. For a few moments he just looked at her, nodding. Liza could barely breathe.

*I know it. I know it. I just know he likes me,* she thought. *He's checking out my look, and he likes it already.*

Liza smiled, praying she looked very booked and very confident.

"You're Liza Ruff."

"Yes," Liza replied, not knowing what else to say.

Bernie rubbed the corner of his chin nervously, continuing to nod. "All the way from the University of Springfield," he added in a singsong voice.

"Ha," Liza tried to joke, slapping her knee a little. "You know it."

Bernie chuckled, as if he were in on the joke, continuing to nod nervously. "And you know my son, Rich."

Liza was beginning to feel there was something a little funny about the meeting. "Yes, I do," she answered. "As you know," she added.

"Uh-*huh.*"

Liza opened her mouth to tell the cute joke about Rich she'd practiced, but there was something strange in his look that made her stop.

"Okay." Bernie stood up and held out his hand good-naturedly. "Let's see the letter."

Liza frowned. "The letter you sent me last week?"

Bernie gave her a reassuring smile. "Yeah. That letter."

Quickly Liza dug into her purse and drew out the letter.

"Hmm," Bernie said slowly, examining the envelope, then pulling out the letter. His eyebrows shot up as he read it. "Oh, good," he exclaimed softly. "That's very good."

Liza was beginning to get a strange, sick feeling. Maybe Travis was right. Maybe she *had* entered the Twilight Zone. Why was he acting this way?

"Liza," Bernie began in a gentle, fatherly tone,

handing the letter back to her over the desk, "I didn't send that letter to you. My son, Rich, did."

"*What?*" Liza cried out in confusion. She stood up like a jack-in-the-box. This wasn't happening. She was going back to the U. of S. with a big, fat contract. She *had* to. She'd never be able to face anyone again if she didn't. Everything inside her was paralyzed. She could barely catch her breath as she stood in the middle of the office, staring at him. "*What?*" she repeated.

Bernie shrugged and gave her a sympathetic look. "Hey, kid. I'm sorry I have to tell you this. Especially after you came all this way. It's a good forgery, but it's not my letterhead and it's definitely not my words."

Liza's lower lip began trembling. Rich really *had* been mad at her. So mad that he'd made a gigantic effort to get back at her. What a cruel joke. Rich was worse than evil. He was a complete and total sicko. She gave Bernie a terrified look. "And the TV show . . ."

"'Greasy Spoon?'" Bernie looked amazed. "I'm awfully sorry, Liza. But I'm afraid he made the whole thing up."

"Oh . . . my . . . God." Liza sank back down into the couch. The rest of her life was going to be complete and total humiliation. She'd have to leave the country for a few years.

"I've been tied up for the last two days. This is the first chance I've had to get you over here, Liza,"

Bernie explained. He took a breath and shook his head sadly. "But I wanted to meet with you personally. Rich's pranks go way, way back. He has a history of devising master schemes for getting back at people he imagines have hurt him in some way."

"Oh," Liza said, numb. "Well, he certainly succeeded."

"He's a complicated kid," Bernie said, sighing. "You know about his stutter, of course. And his mother and I made some mistakes . . ."

"So, you've never seen the tape of my comedy act?" Liza asked quietly.

"No, I haven't," Bernie answered sorrowfully, standing up, as if to signal that the meeting was over. "I'm sorry you had to come such a long way only to be disappointed."

For a moment Liza couldn't think of anything to say. As she stood up, she felt her legs begin to buckle, and hot tears begin to form behind her eyes. She felt as if she might break down right in front of Bernie.

*Don't look desperate, Liza.* She heard Travis's words echo in her head. *They can smell desperation on you like blood.*

Then, slowly, Liza began to straighten up. Travis was right. If she walked out of that office right now in tears, she'd never walk through those doors again.

Liza looked up into Bernie's eyes and took his hand lightly. Then she gripped it harder and began shaking it with enthusiasm. Suddenly she realized that she had nothing to lose and everything to gain by putting on her most lighthearted face. It might just be the toughest acting job of her career. "Hey," she said cheerfully. "Don't give it another thought. That Rich. What a card. He knew I was coming to L.A. to talk with some agents and take care of some auditions. I guess he thought a practical joke was what I needed."

Bernie looked stunned. "What you needed?"

Liza fluffed up her hair and reached for her purse. "Oh, he's always saying my head's getting too big. You know. With all the attention I've been getting since my comedy act came out on that national cable TV show. The phone hasn't stopped ringing."

"Oh. Good. I'm happy for you."

In a burst of inspiration, Liza dug into her purse and pulled out her one and only tape of the show. "Slip it in your VCR and check it out if you have a spare sec. Lots of new talent on it. I'm pretty good, too."

"Thank you." Bernie took the cassette and stared at it thoughtfully.

"No, thank *you!*" Liza impulsively kissed him on one pudgy cheek. "I'm going to give that kid of yours a good kick in the pants when I get back!"

"You be sure to do that," Bernie murmured thoughtfully as Liza rushed out the door. "Maybe you can get through to him."

A few seconds later Liza was rushing down the hallway, convulsed with sobs. She could hear Travis behind her, calling her name, and trying to catch up. But she didn't want to stop, even for the elevator. Spotting an exit sign, Liza yanked open the door to the concrete fire stairs, bolted inside, and sat down on the steps, tears streaming down her cheeks.

She heard the door open and felt Travis sit down quietly next to her. "What happened?" he murmured.

*"IT WAS ALL A PRACTICAL JOKE!"* Liza wailed, leaning her head into his shoulder. *"THERE WAS NO 'GREASY SPOON' SHOW. IT WAS A FAKED LETTER. IT WAS JUST MY SO-CALLED BOYFRIEND GETTING BACK AT ME."*

"Oh, man."

"I've never been so embarrassed," Liza cried. "And all my money . . . gone!"

Travis slid closer to her. He tickled her under her chin a little. Then he turned her wet face toward his. "Stuff like that happens. The world is full of really screwed-up people. Always has been. Always will be."

"That's a depressing way to look at it," Liza snapped. She tore a tissue out of her purse and blew her nose noisily.

"But it's not," Travis insisted, putting his arm around her shoulders. He took off his driver's hat and placed it on the cold concrete step. "You've just got to relax. Expect that a lot of creeps will come your way, then do your best to avoid them. That way you won't be surprised."

Liza sniffed.

"Look. This is what I do when it gets bad."

Liza gave Travis a halfhearted look.

"I drive out to Venice. I run down to the beach. I scream at the waves. I yell at the sky. And I swear at the sand."

"I'm sorry, Travis," Liza said dully, staring at his clean-cut face and long, shaggy hair. "That's not going to make this boo-boo go away."

Travis grabbed her shoulders. "No. But it's going to make you feel a whole lot better. What do you say? A cheap date. Tonight. We'll kick some sand. We'll check out the people. Get weird. Go a little crazy."

Liza stared back, beginning to understand something about Travis. Sure, he was disappointed that her audition was a complete flop. But it didn't matter to him. He actually liked her just for who she was . . . even at her very worst rock bottom. "Okay," she whispered.

"Okay, then."

Liza took Travis's hand, a tear sliding down her cheek. "Thank you, Travis. Thank you."

# Fourteen

..................................................

**F**aith was hurrying across the intersection of Front and Fourth streets, the dingiest corner of Springfield's business district. She blinked her tired, scratchy eyes and fought back the urge to curl up and sleep on a sidewalk bench. Up ahead she could see a bus pulling noisily into the station.

"Winnie!" Faith shouted over her shoulder. She winced. Winnie's heaviest suitcase was pulling her arm out like a piece of taffy. "That could be the Jacksonville bus."

"Okay," Winnie called back, casting a longing glance down the street, as if she were looking for something . . . or someone. The spikes in Winnie's hair were beginning to wilt with her effort of lugging another small suitcase and a backpack.

Faith stopped and looked back worriedly. Winnie was lagging way behind. Her wrinkled tank top was sticking to her skin and one of her running shoes was untied. "Winnie is pregnant," she murmured sympathetically. "I still can't believe it. And all this time she'd been trying to tell me."

"You go ahead," Winnie panted, glancing back down the street again.

Faith raced ahead and pushed open the smudgy glass door leading to the bus station's ticket office. "Excuse me," she asked the woman behind the window, "When's the next bus for Jacksonville?"

"We had a breakdown south of here." The woman looked wearily at her watch. "It'll be here at two-thirty . . . at the earliest."

*"Two-thirty?"* Faith exclaimed, setting the suitcase down with a thud on the dirty linoleum floor. It was only one o'clock now. Her plan had been to rush back to the library, settle on a *Shrew* concept, then do a little cramming before five o'clock for the Western Civ makeup. Now, at best, she'd only have an hour to think about *Shrew* before gearing up for the exam.

*There is no way I can do this,* Faith thought helplessly, sinking down on one of the cracked plastic seats in the waiting room. *But I can't let Winnie down.*

A few moments later, Winnie opened the door slowly and dragged herself in.

"Winnie," Faith finally said as Winnie collapsed next to her. "Are you sure you're doing the right thing?"

"I don't know," Winnie replied dully, raking a hand through her nest of hair. "I mean I *do* know. It's just that I have to do *something*. If I don't, I could go through the entire pregnancy and not ever get to talk to Josh about it. I can see me giving birth and Josh saying, 'Okay, Win. I'm ready to face it. You're pregnant. Let's talk.' Except I won't be pregnant. I'll be a mother by then."

"Winnie . . ." Faith began.

"It's true, it's true," Winnie babbled tearfully. "He's like a robot. A mute. It's a silent movie. He's on the inside of one of those soundproof boxes the TV game show contestants sit in so everyone knows the answer except them."

"Winnie . . ." Faith stared down at a piece of squished chewing gum on the dirty floor. The room smelled of stale popcorn and cigarette smoke. She was trying to focus on Winnie. But all she could think of were her Western Civ dates. *The Taming of the Shrew* set. And Becker's words whispering in her ear: *You are willing to help them with their problems. But they don't give anything back.*

"Josh is like a silent computer chip," Winnie continued to babble. "He functions. You know, he goes to class, he aces his exams, he shops and eats hamburgers and takes showers and talks to people. But he can't feel anything. He isn't capable of expressing emotion."

"Winnie!" Faith cried out, exasperated. "You're not making sense. Josh isn't like that and you know it. You have to talk to him, not run away from him."

Winnie's dark eyes clouded. She closed them and let two large tears slide down her cheeks. "I absolutely won't see him again. I can't. I have to get away from him to sort things out. Hundreds of miles away. I can't be near him right now. You're the only one I need right now, Faith."

Faith looked up as the door to the ticket office opened and Josh's head suddenly appeared. Wearing a faded T-shirt and a two-day stubble, Josh looked exhausted. Faith watched as his anguished eyes shot to Winnie's slumped body. Suddenly he was leaping across the room and scooping Winnie up in his arms. "Winnie, don't go. Please!"

*"JOSH!"* Winnie screamed as if they were reunited wartime lovers. "Oh, Josh." She exclaimed as his head bent down and he pressed his lips tightly to hers.

Faith narrowed her eyes suspiciously. How did Josh find out where Winnie was?

"Winnie, I'm so sorry," Josh said tenderly.

"It's all right. It's all right," Winnie answered, out of breath. "All that matters is that we're together."

Faith's mouth dropped open in shock. What was happening? Two seconds ago, Winnie was determined to get away and let things cool down between her and Josh. Now they were locked into an impossibly long, X-rated kiss.

Josh came up for air, gasping. "I found your notes. I couldn't bear to think of you leaving."

"Oh, Josh," Winnie sobbed.

"What notes?" Faith whispered.

"I know I've been terrible," Josh went on. "I just couldn't handle it. I couldn't think."

"It's okay."

"I'm a dope."

"I love you, you dope."

"How can you love a jerk like me?"

Faith put her hands on her hips and glared from one to the other.

"You're the best thing that's ever happened to me, Josh," Winnie answered, sighing.

"What happened to the one o'clock bus, Win?" Josh asked. "Your note said you were leaving then, and it's a little past that now."

*"You told him you were going?"* Faith cried.

"Well, I . . ." Winnie began, a guilty look crossing her face.

*"YOU EVEN TOLD HIM WHAT TIME THE BUS WAS LEAVING?"* Faith began to yell.

Josh was frowning at Faith and putting Winnie's

backpack on. Then he scooped up all the rest of her luggage with one arm, while Winnie clung to the other.

Faith crossed her arms and stared bitterly at the ancient Coca-Cola poster hanging on the opposite wall. "You knew he would come and stop you. But you just had to drag me along."

"Faith!" Winnie protested. "I needed you. It's a terrible time for us. And thanks to you, well . . ." Winnie sighed happily. "All's well that ends well."

Faith looked at her, seething. "You manipulated me."

Winnie looked shocked. "What?"

"Good old Faith," Faith went on. "Security blanket for rent. No. Not for rent. For free. You knew that this day was a critical one for me. That I'd be losing precious hours on a presentation that could affect my career in the theater if I came down here with you. But you didn't really mean to leave for Jacksonville. It was just a ploy to get Josh to come rescue you."

"Faith," Winnie breathed. "This is a terrible crisis for me. . . ."

Faith nodded. "It is a crisis for you. But I'm in a crisis, too. And you knew that."

"I can't believe this."

"Believe it, Winnie," Faith cried out. "I have been used. I feel sick and tired and used once again by the people I thought were my true friends. Now, if you don't mind, I've got a makeup test and the most important theater idea of my life to dream up. Say good-bye to faithful Faith."

"Six hundred words." Lauren slapped her "His/Her" column copy down on her editor's desk in the *Journal* newsroom. "Seven P.M. Thursday. On the dot, I might add. And it's in the hard drive under the code word PIG."

Greg Sukamaki looked up from the piles on his desk. Nearby him were other writers and copy editors—either bent intently at their computer screens, aiming wadded up pieces of paper at their wastebaskets, or staring grumpily into space. Greg folded his arms on top of a stack of papers and squinted his eyes at her. "Gee, Lauren. It's nice to see you, too."

"What do you want?" Lauren said irritably. Her tight black T-shirt read: "Anita Hill was telling the truth," and her red parachute pants hung loosely about her shrinking waist. "I stayed up all night on this piece. Do you want me to sit on your lap or something?"

"No, thank you, Lauren," Greg replied with mock patience.

Lauren flopped down on a chair next to Greg's desk, and crossed her legs. "Okay, so sue me."

"If this 'His/Her' column weren't so unbelievably popular, I'd pull you and Dash off the assignment,"

Greg said with a half smile. "You two are a couple of nut cases every week."

Lauren's head was buzzing with fury. She clenched her fists in her pants pockets and bit the side of her lip. "Dash comes up with stuff out of nowhere," she barked. "He looks at my copy and starts spouting off about my so-called 'arrogant, oh-so-serious-above-it-all tone.' You know. When I talk about feminism."

"Oooooo. Ouch," Greg cracked. Then he sat back in his chair and stared into her eyes. "You could tone it down a little, Lauren." He held up his thumb and forefinger to show a tiny space between them. "Just a bit."

"Then he goes on and on about how I build walls," she started, then stopped, frustrated. "You don't want to hear this." Lauren stared off at a distant point. She could feel something coiling inside her chest like a spring that was ready to snap.

"There's Angry Woman herself." Lauren heard a voice behind her.

Lauren stiffened. Dash. That was all she needed. She couldn't bear it when he put on his macho, tough-guy act around her. It was irritating. She just knew him too well. And she knew he was only acting that way to show off for Greg. Lauren heaved a sigh and looked back at Dash smirking at her as he leaned against the edge of a desk nearby.

"Hey," Lauren snapped back. "Mr. Sensitive in the flesh. Get a chance to check the spelling errors you spread so generously throughout your column?"

"Lauren," Greg said quietly. "The computer will catch typos."

"You're forgetting, Greg," Dash spat. "Lauren is the product of a long string of snotty boarding schools. And that's where they really know how to teach letter-perfect spelling. Word-perfect grammar. Everything just so. Except they don't ever teach them how to think."

"Who did teach me how to think then, Dash?" Lauren fumed. "You've been relying on my ideas all year long. Where did you think they came from? Cliff Notes?"

She grabbed her purse, slung it over her shoulder, and gave Dash a hard look. "He's slipping, Greg. Now I'm going to get some rest, preferably someplace as far away as possible from this place."

As she rushed up the basement stairs to the main floor of the U. of S.'s bustling student union, Lauren felt her anger rise up like a plume of smoke.

"What nerve!" she said through clenched teeth as she stalked across the dorm green toward Forest Hall. Its lawn and courtyard swarmed with Frisbee players, joggers doing warm-up stretches, and a few students straggling in from late classes. Loud music was blasting from a speaker poised on a second story window, and a water balloon fight had just erupted near the door.

She looked up at the gray thunderclouds rolling up

over the distant mountains. The air had a heavy, wet feel to it, and she could almost feel the distant raindrops.

As she drew closer, the music got louder, and her nerves got tighter. She'd always hated Forest Hall, the jock dorm, and the mindless, stupid creeps who lived there. The crazy parties. The practical jokes.

"Coming through!" Lauren screamed, causing the water balloon throwers to abruptly stop. Shoving the glass door open, she ran up the stairway, silently praying that Melissa would be gone somewhere. Anywhere. The weight room. The library. The moon.

When she reached the door to her dorm room, her heart sank. Inside, she could hear familiar grunting sounds. She opened the door and stared angrily at her roommate.

"Hey," Melissa grunted, looking up briefly from her sit-ups. Lauren didn't move. She just continued to stare at Melissa as if she were an alien being. Her feet planted on a thin exercise pad, Melissa brought her elbows up to her knees at a speed Lauren never thought was possible. Up and down. Up and down. Melissa's face was slightly pink and wet strands of hair were beginning to stick to her forehead, but she didn't stop and she didn't even slow her amazing pace.

"Hi," Lauren answered, about to burst with frustration. She just stood there, not knowing whether to stay or go. If Melissa planned to exercise all evening again, she'd never get to sleep. She was trapped.

Melissa kept bobbing up and down like a robot with a messed-up electrical system. "Are you planning on standing there all night, or will you be coming in?" Melissa grunted.

"Melissa." Lauren planted a hand on her hip. "Not for the world. Not for the world." With that, she turned and fled out into the noisy hall, leaving the door wide open.

For a few minutes Lauren paced in the hallway to let off steam. She was tired. She was upset. Her nerves were frayed from staying up all night writing and thinking about Dash. If only she could find a quiet corner to curl up in, she knew she'd fall asleep immediately. She didn't care where it was. The hall. The basement. The bushes.

Bolting back down the stairs, Lauren spotted a jock in a crew cut opening his mouth and belching loudly at no one in particular. She balled up her fists and briefly considered delivering him a basic shin kick and instep stomp. Outside, she kicked the plastic trash at the front door, sending it into the bushes.

Lauren stormed past the Frisbee players again and thought about her old room with Faith in Coleridge Hall. It wasn't a completely quiet dorm. But when people made noise there, it was usually because they were practicing a beautiful piece of music or rehearsing lines for a show.

Suddenly, Lauren stopped. Quickly, she dug into

her purse and pulled out an old dorm key she'd reported lost many months ago, but which had turned up again.

Digging her heels into the grass, Lauren took off across the dorm green toward Coleridge Hall. Raindrops were starting to fall and she heard a distant rumble and sudden crack of thunder. By the time she reached the front entrance, the rain was coming down in torrents. She could hear squeals of surprise all over the dorm green as people ran for shelter. At last she reached her old room, knocked softly, then let herself in.

"Thank God," Lauren mumbled to herself, flopping down on her old bed in the dim light. The rainwater was pouring down in comforting streams on the old-fashioned windowpanes. "This is the only place in Springfield that's ever given me a moment of peace." Her eyelids were already beginning to droop as she curled up on Liza's bed and glanced happily across at Faith's side of the room. She always loved to look across at her clutter of photographs, theater souvenirs, and scripts.

"Liza's probably still away and Faith won't mind," Lauren thought sleepily, closing her eyes and drifting off to sleep. "At least Faith won't mind. Kind, generous Faith. She'd give her right arm just to help a friend like me. I just know she would . . ."

# Fifteen

**L**iza dug her heels into the packed sand and stared at the waves collapsing and slipping toward her on the sunny beach. Farther out, the ocean was a smooth mirror of blue that stretched calmly to meet the sky.

She'd never seen anything so big. And she'd never felt so small.

Liza tightened the scarf around her head and hugged herself against the cool breeze. A few minutes before, she and Travis had driven to the section of L.A. called Venice Beach and had rushed down the wooden steps to the oceanfront. She was grateful to Travis for keeping the promise to give her a wonderful, wild last night in Los Angeles—especially after her disastrous meeting with Bernie Greenberg.

But even though Travis had immediately headed wildly for the water, something made Liza hold back. This impossibly huge beach wasn't anything like the beaches near Brooklyn that were more like acres of bodies and snack bars. This beach was big. It was empty. And it made her feel strange.

"At least get your toes wet!" She could hear Travis yelling happily at her.

Liza squinted at his wet head and chest bobbing in the water. He was waving at her, splashing, and howling at the sky as if he didn't have a care in the world. It almost made Liza want to pretend she didn't, either. But she didn't know if she could. After all, she'd just been through the most terrible, humiliating experience of her life. And the next morning she'd be headed back to the U. of S., where she'd have to explain everything to everyone she blabbed to before she left.

The mere thought of facing her friends again made her sick to her stomach.

*Everyone is going to laugh in my face. And I won't even get to run out and buy something to wear to feel better,* she moaned silently. *Because on top of everything else, I'm broke.*

"Come on," Travis was yelling again. "If you don't come in, I'm going to get you!"

Liza's eyes opened with alarm as she saw him begin to run out of the churning water toward her. She bit her lip and began to step back slowly as Travis got closer. She could see his lively blue eyes and the water streaming off his hair onto his wet chest.

"Come on, Liza," Travis teased, his baggy shorts sagging around the waist. "I want ten wet toes. Now!"

Liza stepped back faster and began to hop on one foot as she unfastened a sandal. "Travis," she warned.

"Liza!" Travis yelled dramatically, opening his arms and running toward her.

"*AAAHHHHH!*" Liza screamed, sending a thrill up her spine. Quickly, she ripped off her red sandals and began running down the beach to her left. "*AHHHHHH!*" She couldn't resist screaming again.

"*AHHHHHHH!*" Travis replied.

"*AHHHHHHH!*" Liza screamed louder as she raced down the hard, wet sand, feeling the muscles in her legs begin to work. Her lungs took in buckets of clean air. Her heart beat mightily. And the wind blew in her hair. She was alive. She hadn't felt this free since she was a little girl.

"*WHHOOOOAAA.*" Travis tried to swoop down on her, but Liza dug her heel into the sand and playfully changed direction, narrowly missing his grasp.

"*AHHHHHHHHHH!*" She yelled at the top of her lungs, laughing hysterically. No one heard her.

No one cared. Nothing mattered. It was just her and Travis in the middle of the world. Specks on the planet. Bernie Greenberg's next show could be a complete and total flop. Hollywood could disappear in the smog. Every member of the U. of S. student body could laugh at her. But the waves would keep rolling. The sun would keep shining and the clouds would keep floating by.

"Got you!" Travis grabbed Liza by the waist and picked her up.

Liza screamed. She giggled and kicked. Travis was carrying her in a slow trot down the beach toward the water.

*"STOPPPP!"* She yelled it again, just before he did and lowered her toes gently into the foamy swirl of water that had just swept under them.

"Feels good, doesn't it?" Travis was grinning at her over his shoulder. His face was very tanned and wet. The small gold ring in his ear glinted in the last rays of sun.

Liza smiled back, leaning into the wet skin of his shoulders and torso as he set her down in shallower water. "Yes, it does, Travis. And thank you very, very much."

"Let's run," Travis sang out, as Liza untied her head scarf and shook out her hair in the breeze.

"Race you!" Liza yelled, starting off down the wide, empty stretch.

A while later, after a long walk down the beach and back, Liza and Travis had dug themselves into a hollow of sand and watched the people Rollerblading on the busy boardwalk nearby. Liza's damp head was nestled comfortably in Travis's elbow. For once in her life, she didn't feel the need to say anything. Not a word.

"Look at that," Liza finally whispered, gazing at the wet stretch of beach left by the falling tide. The sun had begun to sink, so that the shiny sand gradually became a mirror reflecting the orange sky and clouds.

"Yeah." Travis sighed. "Makes you wonder what we get so worked up about back there. This is what's really happening."

"Uh-huh." Liza sighed deeply.

They shared a happy silence as the light settled. A few seagulls flew lazily above. The constant sweep and roar of the waves made Liza feel drowsy and relaxed and very, very happy.

"Travis?"

"Liza?"

"I never did tell you why Rich Greenberg went to the trouble of sabotaging me."

"No." Travis looked down at her. "I guess you never did."

Liza took a deep breath. "Rich was in the same comedy competition I was at the U. of S. That was how I met him. And we started seeing each other a little." She curled her legs up, and nestled closer to Travis. "Anyway, the night before the big contest, he didn't meet me for a date we had planned, and I got mad. I mean, I got red-hot mad.

"How mad?" Travis joked.

Liza jabbed him in the ribs. "So . . . the next day, I just happened to stumble upon the dummy he was using for his ventriloquist act. And I hid it."

"Liza. You baaaaad."

"I know. I deserved everything that happened to me this week." Liza shook her head guiltily. "He had to drop out of the competition. Anyway, he found out about it and pretended everything was still fine between us. But he was hatching this plan the whole time. I didn't even realize it."

Travis frowned. "You didn't sense that anything was wrong?"

Liza shrugged. She felt her eyes begin to sting a little. "I guess I was so desperate to believe he liked me, that I overlooked a few warning signs." Liza cocked her head a little and smiled. "Like how he never laughed at my jokes and was usually as cool as a Popsicle around me."

Travis shook his head. "Man, you *were* desperate. Why?"

Liza looked at him. "Because I *was*. Because I always have been. Look at me, Travis." Liza twisted around and faced him. "Look at this nose. Look at this dopey face and this pudgy body. In high school, I was worse. By about twenty-five pounds. No one ever asked me out."

"Are you kidding?" Travis looked amazed.

"So what do you think I did to get attention?" Liza cracked. "Sit still and try to look pretty? No. I dyed my hair, pretended I was Bette Midler, told stupid jokes, and always made sure to do all the talking. Real loud. So no one could have a chance to tell me to shut up. You wouldn't have stood me five seconds in high school."

Travis took Liza's chin between his thumb and his forefinger. Then, slowly and tenderly he turned her face toward his. "I don't really care what they said in high school."

"Really?" Liza whispered, unable to meet his eyes.

"I think you're beautiful, Liza Ruff, inside and out. And you're fun and smart," Travis murmured, his long hair rustling in the breeze.

"I am?" Liza replied, weak.

"You have style." Travis slipped his arm around her shoulder and looked out to the ocean. "Think about the way you handled Bernie this morning, for instance. You didn't rush out of his office in tears. You came up with an incredible face-saver. You gave him your tape. Instead of making him feel guilty, you made him curious. It was an amazing save. You probably made him want to see you again. How many other people could do that?"

Liza felt tears begin to well up in her eyes, then spill down her cheeks. "You were the one who told me how to act."

Liza felt Travis's hand pull her close. She looked up at the shadow of his face for a moment, then felt his lips drop down and brush hers.

This wasn't a script. Travis's feelings were real. Liza didn't have to think things through. Or even learn any punch lines. For the first time in her life, all she had to do was just enjoy the moment. This single moment in time. The best moment of the best day of her life.

# Sixteen

"Thank you, Seattle Shakespeare Festival." Becker smiled to himself, rolling a dime into the photocopy machine. "Your western-style production of *Taming of the Shrew* is ripe for the taking."

It was eight o'clock Thursday night in the empty periodical section of the U. of S. library. That morning, Faith's panic had shot up into the danger zone after sleeping through her Western Civ exam. Plus, she still hadn't come up with a *Shrew* idea.

But at last, he'd found it.

After two hours of desperate searching through the microfilm machine, he finally found a western-style

Shakespearean production concept Faith could use for her presentation the next day.

"Thank you, *New York Times* regional theater critic, for reviewing it," Becker murmured, sticking another dime into the machine and sighing happily. "I almost feel as if I'd watched the show. In fact, I almost feel as if it were my idea. Or, rather, *Faith's* idea."

Becker looked up at the ceiling and groaned with happiness. "Here it is. *Shrew* in the wild West," Becker muttered to himself, his eyes hungrily scanning the article. "All described in a lengthy 'Arts & Leisure' section chronicle. The sets. The costumes. The tone. Even detailed explanations of how key passages were delivered by the actors nearly fifteen years before."

Becker slipped the precious photocopies into his black notebook and put away his tiny round glasses. Then he stuffed everything into his huge book bag and headed down the library stairs past the checkout points and outside.

There was a loud thunderclap as Becker stepped across the library courtyard and hurried onto the dorm green. He could feel steady raindrops begin to fall onto his head, and in the evening light he could see a heavy sheet of rain sweeping across the campus.

Becker smiled and tucked his book bag under his arm. "It's a sign," he cried softly. "The heavens have opened up! Faith is almost mine. She'll love me for this. We'll share our lives. Our thoughts. Everything."

Bending his head against the torrent of rain, Becker began to plan.

He'd explain that the idea had come to him in the children's section of the library. Faith liked little kids. He'd tell her he looked at some antique cowboys and Indians books—and bingo, thought of it himself.

After a few minutes, he could see the yellow lights of Coleridge Hall blazing out through the rain. Becker smiled. This was the idea that would land Faith a spot in the drama program. He was certain of it. And once she did, Faith would never be able to thank him enough. "She'll trust *me*, not her crazy, selfish friends," he said aloud.

By the time Becker neared the dorm entrance, water was streaming down his face and soaking into his clothes. He had to see Faith. He needed her. Faith was the one person who could fill the hole in his life. Only she could melt away the awkwardness and the strange feeling he always carried with him that he was alone, different . . . unwanted.

When he reached the room, Becker slid his key in the doorknob and slowly unlocked the door.

His heart sank. Faith was gone.

Becker sighed and slowly lowered his book bag to the floor, deciding not to turn on the lights. Then he slipped his hands in his pockets and walked over to the window.

Rain. Alone with the rain.

But as he stared at the rivulets of water trickling down the pane, he thought he detected a faint sound behind him. The sound of something rustling, or perhaps . . . someone breathing?

Becker swung around and squinted in the darkness. What was that?

He took a step forward and looked at his bed. A shiver of excitement flew up his neck. There, underneath the sheet of *his* bed, someone lay sound asleep. A few strands of blond hair trailed out over the covers.

Faith?

Becker took a step closer, his heart melting like butter. In the dim light he could barely make out the curve of her body under the sheet. He could hear her soft breathing.

Was it Faith?

Slowly Becker peeled off his rainsoaked shirt and let it drop to the floor.

In his bed?

He gazed at the silky hair. Obviously, she couldn't wait. She wanted him now. She wanted to show him how much she cared. Without words. Without confusion.

Becker knelt down by the bed, his bare chest lightly touching the sheet. Desire was flooding through him, making him dizzy. Making him afraid. He hadn't planned on this. He needed a few seconds to adjust. His plan was to wait until the end of the dorm experiment. Then Faith would realize how much she loved and missed him.

But this? Now?

This was too much.

His heart swelling, his fingertips tingling, Becker ran his hand down the curve of her back under the sheet. Then he lowered his head and nuzzled her soft hair. Finally, he drew down the sheet a little so that he could touch his lips to hers . . .

*"AAAAGGHHHHHHHHHH!"* Becker heard an ear-splitting scream.

The next second, something hard connected with his face in the darkness.

*"OOOHHHH!"* Becker staggered back. A searing pain shot through his nose and into his head. "FAITH? What are you doing?"

*"YYYYYEEEEYYYYYAAAAAAHHHHH-HH!"* The high-pitched scream tore through the darkness once again. "GET OUT!"

Becker stumbled forward, trying to orient himself in the darkness. Then, without warning, a leg seemed to lock around his ankle and a solidly-built hip slammed into the front of his body. His body crashed to the floor.

"Faith? Faith?" Becker cried out through his pain. "Is that you? What have I done?"

"Ugh!" He heard someone grunt.

*"AAAUUUUUGGGGGGGHHHHH!"* Becker

groaned. An elbow jabbed him in the stomach.

"Take that, sucker!" a woman's voice was yelling just before he felt the side of an iron-hard hand in his stomach.

Becker began trying to grab the thrashing figure, trying to ignore the pain and the spinning in his head. In the background, he could vaguely hear someone pounding on the door, but he was trying to concentrate on controlling the wild animal that kept lunging at him in the darkness.

He grabbed a leg, and pulled someone to the ground with a thud. There was thrashing. A painful kick to the shoulder.

*Who is this?* Becker thought desperately as he grabbed at the air, trying to hang onto something, trying to make the person stop. Was it Faith? Liza? Brooks? One of Faith's other insane friends?

Suddenly, the door burst open and there was a block of dim light. He could hear people shouting around him.

"*HELP!*" he heard the voice scream again. The thrashing stopped.

Becker fell back helplessly. There were people everywhere now. The sound of a gathering crowd at the door. Confusion. Searing pain. "What's— going—on?" he could barely whisper.

All of a sudden the overhead lights flashed on. He looked up, trying to see through the pain and nausea. Milling above him were dozens of concerned pairs of eyes.

"What happened?" yelled Kimberly, who had rushed in from her room next door and was clinging protectively to a familiar-looking woman with disheveled hair and blazing, violet eyes.

Becker looked up, shielding his eyes from the light. "I'm not sure . . ." he gasped.

"He attacked me!" the woman with the violet eyes shrieked, pointing at Becker.

Becker looked up in confusion. "Who . . . who are you?"

"What do you mean—who am I?" the woman screamed. Becker recognized her now. She was Lauren. One of Faith's friends. Fully dressed in camouflage pants and a black tank top, she was breathing hard. Her mouth was like a single, taut line of sheer aggression. "What difference does it make who I am? You attacked me!"

"What are you doing here?" Becker sputtered.

"I was resting in Faith's room!" Lauren yelled, hunching her shoulders hysterically, acting as if she were going to attack again.

"Stop, Lauren!" Kimberly held her back.

"You can't do that!" Becker tried to prop himself up on his elbow. Something sticky and warm was running down his face.

Lauren tried to lunge at him, but several people

restrained her. "I don't care what you think! You pulled the sheet off and tried to attack me!"

*"You are crazy!"* Becker screamed.

Suddenly he heard a familiar voice at the door and saw someone pushing through the crowd.

"Becker!" Faith cried out, her eyes darting around the room, terrified. "What happened?"

Becker tried to stand up. He wished he could throttle Lauren. She was just standing there as if she had a perfect right to. "This so-called friend of yours . . . has punched me in the face . . . kicked me in the—"

Faith was looking around wildly. "What? Who? What happened?"

"Lauren decided to have a little rest in my bed, so—"

"Lauren?" Faith was yelling. "What's this have to do with Lauren? Huh?"

"He attacked me!" Lauren yelled back.

Faith looked confused. "Someone get some ice!" she yelled to the group at the door. She grabbed a box of tissues and handed it to him.

Becker sat up a little and pressed a wad of tissues to his nose. "I guess Lauren thought I was an intruder."

Faith looked up sharply. Her face was haggard and there were gray circles under her eyes. "Lauren did this to you?"

"He attacked me!" Lauren spat. "I had to defend myself."

Faith stood up and stared at Lauren, her eyes blazing with fury. "What were *you* doing here?"

"I found my old key . . ." Lauren mumbled, her fists tightly clenched, glaring at Becker. "I needed a quiet place to get some rest—"

*"You needed what?"* Faith suddenly screamed. Lauren's mouth snapped shut and her eyes opened wide. *"Are you insane?* I cannot believe this. Get out. I've had enough of you and all my friends. Who do you guys think I am? A doormat? Someone who deserves absolutely no consideration or courtesy? How dare you barge into my room, then attack my roommate?"

Becker drew in his breath a little. Desperately he tried to hold back the victorious smile that was forming on his lips.

Maybe this episode was going to help him. Maybe Faith was finally realizing something. Maybe now she'd finally get rid of her friends.

"But, Faith . . ." Lauren pleaded, backing out the door. "I didn't exactly barge in, I didn't think you'd mind."

*"Of course you didn't,"* Faith cried out, pushing the wisps of her now-scraggly braid off her face as she backed Lauren and the rest of the crowd out of the door. "You are so used to taking advantage of me that of course you wouldn't think I'd mind. You and all my so-called friends. Winnie. Brooks. You're all

crazy and selfish. I don't need friends like you. Believe me. I really don't."

With that, Faith slammed the door on Lauren's frightened face. Then she turned around and dove onto her bed, sobbing.

*Victory is finally mine,* Becker thought.

For a while he sat on the edge of Faith's bed, squeezing her hand and dabbing his bloody nose. Outside, the rain lashed against the windowpane and the wind was rushing in the elms. Faith finally flipped over and looked at him. Her eyes were so intense, Becker thought they were going to bore a hole through him. "Are you okay?"

Becker thrilled. "Yeah."

Faith looked desperate. Her blue eyes were puffy and filled with tears. Her mouth was trembling and her hands were shaking a little. "I can't take this much longer, Becker," she breathed, looking away. "I have to get away from them."

"Let me take you away," Becker whispered, staring down at the lovely shape of her face and the smooth curve of her neck.

Faith touched his cheek. Her face was very serious. "I'm ready."

Becker could barely breathe. She was so close he wanted to melt into her. "We belong together."

"I know," Faith whispered, lifting her face up. She snaked a slim arm up around his neck and pulled him down. Then she pressed her lips to his.

"Faith . . ." Becker said softly, before he kissed her. He could feel her fingers on his neck. She was pulling him forward so that he was lying next to her. He kissed her again and felt her body press up against his tightly.

Everything was complete.

Faith was his—at last.

"I need you, Becker," Faith said with an urgent look.

Becker sank down and buried his lips on Faith's neck. "Oh, God, Faith. I need you, too. We need each other."

"I want you . . ." Faith trailed off. She touched the side of his face and gave him a meaningful look.

Becker was burning.

He gazed at her beautiful body on the bed next to him. But he held back. It was too early. Faith needed to be done with *Shrew*. Then she'd really know what he'd done for her.

"Not now," Becker said.

"I need you . . ."

"You already have me," Becker murmured. "But you need the theater, too. I have an idea for *Shrew*. Let's get tomorrow out of the way. Then we'll have all the time we need for each other."

Faith's eyes were burning into his. "You're right."

"For now," Becker murmured in her ear, "we can take our beds and pull them together. It will be wonderful. We'll hold each other close all night long."

# Seventeen

"**A**ll set?" Travis slammed the trunk of the limo and grinned at Liza. He rubbed his hands together gleefully. "All ready to return to campus? Term papers? Exams? Pop quizzes?"

Liza smoothed back her ponytail and grinned at him. "Don't remind me, Travis. Don't remind me. All I need is a good reason to leave my wholesome life in the mountains, and I'll be down here in a flash."

Slipping into the limousine, Liza felt a pang. It wasn't just that she was going back to the U. of S. completely humiliated and ashamed. She didn't want to leave Travis behind.

Travis opened the door for her and bowed with a

flourish. "I can think of one good reason for you to come back."

"Travis." Liza looked at him, trying not to cry. She put on an expression of mock severity. "The reason has to involve money, my dear. You know what I mean? Like a job? Like how else could I afford to live here? The place sucks money right out of your wallet like a high-tech vacuum cleaner."

"I'll be waiting."

Liza felt her heart drop. The night before, after their long walk on the Venice Beach, they'd taken the long way back to the Tropicana Motel. Travis had taken her out for a two o'clock in the morning breakfast at the International House of Pancakes. For two solid hours they drank coffee, ate, and talked. She'd never done that before with a guy.

No jokes. No silly flirting. Just straight talking.

Before Travis, Liza had never believed anyone could like her just for herself. She always thought being loved was all tied up with the way she looked. Or how much she said. She needed to beg for it. With the brightest hair. The loudest clothes. The funniest joke.

Now she knew it was an act. A good act. But still an act.

Travis had taught her that.

"Just don't ever let me see you in that silly cap again," Liza cracked.

Travis pretended to look shocked. He took off his

black limo-driver's cap and examined it. "This? You don't like it?" he mocked.

"Come on, doll." Liza crossed her legs. "Let's go. I'm trying to act like I'm not desperately wishing I could stay. Remember? I wouldn't want you to think I liked you or anything."

"Cool." Travis was only half joking as he shut the car door.

Liza grew silent as the limo left Sunset Boulevard and headed toward the freeway to the airport. Hollywood was a hard place. A tough and dirty place. The revelation about Rich Greenberg's dirty trick had been the worst moment of her life. But how could she complain? Travis had given her the *best* day of her life.

The fact was, the place was tugging at her.

Liza was staring at Travis as he turned onto Aviation Boulevard and began following the airport signs. By now, the smog was thicker than ever and the planes roaring overhead were terrifyingly loud. But she really didn't want to go. Travis was the most wonderful guy she'd ever met. And she'd only had a few short days with him. It didn't seem fair.

"Thanks for everything, Travis," Liza said in a low voice. "I guess I'm too embarrassed to tell you what you've meant to me."

Travis smiled. "I don't want to admit it either."

"What?" Liza was looking at his soft, brown hair and warm, open face.

"What you've meant to *me*."

"Really?" Liza gasped.

Travis shrugged. "Yeah. Sure. What are you talking about?"

"You mean . . . I'm right about thinking . . . that you, uh, really like me?"

Travis looked away from the traffic for a moment with a serious face. Then he reached out and touched her face. "Yes. You're right."

Liza knew she was going to cry.

"It's strange," Travis went on. "You were the one who told me that Winnie got married."

Liza gulped. "Yeah, like a bulldozer I told you."

"Yeah, you delivered the bad news but the strange thing is—you were the one who made me get over her."

Liza gazed at him with tears in her eyes. "Thanks for saying that." She was on the verge of throwing herself on his shoulder when the car phone rang suddenly.

"Yes?" Travis answered. His face grew serious and then he looked over at Liza, stunned. "Yes, she is." He handed her the phone. "It's for you."

Liza looked at him.

"Take it."

"It's for me?"

"Go on." Travis laughed. "Take it. You're not going to believe it."

"Who is it?" Liza hissed, grabbing the receiver and covering the mouthpiece with her hand.

Travis smiled. "It's Bernie Greenberg. The White Line Limo number had been jotted down on the resume you left with him."

Liza froze. *Bernie Greenberg?* The blood began to beat in her head and her palm was getting sweaty just holding the phone. Was he going to sue her for something? Or . . . did he . . . maybe . . . watch her tape?

"Remember," Travis reminded her. "You're hot. You're in demand."

Liza looked away, took a deep breath, and threw back her head. Whatever it was he wanted, she was going to be prepared. She was strong now. "Bernie!" she cried into the receiver. "Glad you got me! You wouldn't believe my schedule today!"

"Yeah, yeah," Bernie answered quickly. "Hey, listen. I saw the tape. Some good stuff there. You were good. Very good."

Tears sprang into Liza's eyes and began rolling like a joyful flood down her face. This was too much happiness. It was more than she ever, ever, could have hoped for. She tried to control the quaver in her voice. "Thank you so *much*. Coming from you, that's a real compliment."

"Listen," Bernie continued in an urgent tone. "We're shooting an episode of 'Belvedere Heights' tomorrow and we were hoping you could make a short appearance on the show. It's only a small part, but . . ."

"Oh!" Liza's voice practically cracked in two. "Excuse

me, Bernie, just a moment, I have another call." Liza stabbed a nail down on the red "Hold" button and grabbed Travis's shoulder. "Oh, my God. Bernie wants me to be on the 'Belvedere Heights' shoot tomorrow," she gushed. "On a show! An actual TV show! The show about those kids who have tons of problems even though their parents are rolling in money."

"Don't keep him on hold too long," Travis said calmly. "You're pushing your luck."

"Bernie!" Liza stabbed the "Hold" button again. "Sorry about that. Of course. I think it would be marvelous. Now let me see what my schedule is tomorrow."

"We'll need you at about ten," Bernie went on. "It's an underfive. Under five lines. And we'll pay union scale. Only a few bucks. Four, five hundred at best. But we've got some pretty funny material for you to play with and the exposure's good. You're gonna play a salesgirl in a department store the kids are trying to scam."

"Sounds good," Liza replied, happiness rushing through her like an out-of-control freight train. "What a kick. That would be fine. Yes. Uh-huh. I'm free then. What luck!"

"Check in at the lot a little before ten," Bernie went on rapidly. "I'll give your name to the security guard and he'll show you where to go."

"Fine!"

"Oh, and I'll have the wardrobe mistress call you

at your hotel this afternoon to get your size for the fitting."

Liza's face was collapsed against the passenger window now but she was determined to stay cool. "Lovely! Thanks much, Bernie! Bye!" Liza hung up the phone.

*"YES!"* Liza screamed into the windshield, holding her head with both hands.

*"AAAHHHHHHHH!"* Travis joined in, pulling the limo off to the side of the road, and grabbing her in a bear hug.

*"AAAAHHHHHHHH!"* Travis and Liza screamed together.

"I can't believe it," Liza cried, her face completely wet now and her mascara dripping down her cheeks. "This is the most wonderful place. Dreams really do come true here, don't they?"

"Yeah, they sure do," Travis agreed, holding her face tenderly and kissing her. "If you have enough faith, they do."

Josh was looking into his coffee cup as if it held the meaning of life. "The strange thing is, Win, it only took a few minutes to get pregnant. A few minutes. But it changed our lives forever."

Winnie bit a corner of her lip. After Josh had picked her up at the bus station on his motorcycle, they had buzzed over to their favorite off-campus coffee house for their long-overdue talk. Winnie's whole body was flooded with relief. At last, Josh was with her. At last, he was talking. Even Faith's strange reaction at the bus station couldn't diminish the joy she felt now.

"I know," Winnie agreed. "I mean, we do a lot of things each day. And a lot of things have consequences. But nothing like *this*."

Josh nodded. "You skip class and your grades go down."

"You eat a half-gallon of chocolate chip ice cream every night for a week and don't run and you gain five pounds," Winnie added, looking deep into Josh's dark eyes. "You spend all your money and you're broke."

Josh shook his head. "The only thing I can compare it to is maybe getting drunk and killing someone on the highway. Now that's a consequence."

"That's much worse than what we're going through," Winnie said, frowning. "Much worse, Josh. When did you suddenly start having such horrible, dark thoughts?"

"I don't know," Josh said. "I know I'm weird these days. I can't help it. We've done a lot of growing up in a very short time. I'm in shock, I guess."

Winnie looked with love at his single tiny blue earring and the woven band he wore around his strong wrist. Josh reached out both hands and covered Winnie's. "But you're right, Win. It's not the end of the world. In fact it could be the best thing that's happened to us."

"I'm so glad we're talking, Josh," Winnie said in a small voice. Until that moment, she didn't know if she'd ever truly understood what being married to Josh meant to her. Now she knew. It was everything. It was right. It wasn't just a fun thing they did one night in Nevada. Marriage and commitment were what they both needed and wanted. "I've felt so alone. So guilty. It was *my* fault we forgot the birth control that one time."

Josh gave her a half-smile and looked into her eyes, sending little goose bumps up and down Winnie's back. "It was my fault, too. I should have backed off when I saw that you weren't really sure if it was safe. I'm sorry, Win. I'm really sorry."

Winnie sighed and took a sip of her herbal tea. "Well, it was a beautiful afternoon."

Josh was struggling. "I know I've been avoiding this conversation. It's just that I haven't been able to shake the thought that we're too young to be parents. We've got college to finish. Adventures ahead of us. We need jobs and incomes and a home we'd want our child to grow up in. I just kept wishing it hadn't happened."

Winnie's heart was breaking inside. She couldn't bear to see Josh this unhappy. And it was all her fault. Well, at least half her fault, anyway. Still, she knew neither of them could afford to wallow in self-doubt and fear. It was time to take action. And if Josh wasn't going to, she was going to be the one.

"But it *did* happen, Josh," Winnie reminded him. "It did happen. I am pregnant. Soon, we're going to have a baby to care for."

Josh was nodding. He took a quick sip of coffee and pulled something out of his backpack.

Winnie stared up at the ceiling, trying to sort her thoughts. "I know it's hard to imagine what lies ahead, because having a baby seems so abstract right now. Sort of like an idea, rather than something that is actually going to happen. But it is, Josh. Think about it. Do you know how much diapers cost?"

Josh was flipping through a booklet.

"When I was at the playground this week, I talked to a woman who told me that it costs almost twenty dollars to buy a package of sixty diapers and they only last a little over a week, Josh," Winnie went on.

"Win—" Josh began.

"She said that it's illegal to put the baby in the car without a special seat and that costs about sixty dollars," Winnie interrupted. "Day-care runs at least five hundred dollars a month and apparently you need to get a family insurance policy to pay for the baby doctor, but it's really hard to get, and . . ." Winnie shrugged, then grinned. "Do you understand?"

Josh stared at her. "Yes. That's why I left so early this morning. I did a little research."

Winnie's mouth dropped open. "Research on what?"

"Oh, everything, really," Josh said matter-of-factly. "There must be a lot of people our age in this situation, because the U. of S. has all kinds of programs for students with kids." Josh started slapping down brochures on the table. "Family housing. Great day-care program on campus. Low-interest loans to help meet tuition and family expenses."

"You got this stuff?" Winnie gasped. She'd been breaking her heart worrying and Josh had actually been doing something.

"Well, yeah," Josh said simply. "You're not the only grown-up around here."

Winnie took his hand. She'd never loved Josh as much as she did at that moment. "That's why you were gone when I came back from the park early this morning? While I was sticking desperate little Post-It notes all over the house, you were doing something constructive?"

"I guess." Josh looked at her. "It's about time, huh?"

"Oh, Josh." Winnie grabbed his other hand and kissed them both. "I'm sorry I gave you such a hard time. Here all I could think about was you. And you were out there thinking about the baby—our family."

"Well," Josh looked down guiltily. "I started thinking about it at four o'clock this morning, anyway."

"I never was planning to leave you," Winnie admitted, letting her face fall. "I couldn't even imagine going back to Jacksonville and living with my mom through all of this. Faith's going to kill me the next time she sees me. I dragged her down to the bus station at sort of a bad time, I guess."

"She'll forgive you," Josh said, reaching over and brushing a spike of hair off her forehead.

Winnie sighed. "It's not easy being married. I mean, it's good. But it's not what it's like in the movies. You know. Romantic bliss for the rest of your life."

"I'm glad we didn't have one of those weddings." Josh wrinkled his nose. "Somehow, I could never picture you in traditional lace and orange blossoms."

"Nah." Winnie was grinning. "I'm not the romantic type, am I? When you think of me, think of someone firmly planted in reality. Scrubbing the bathtub. Dumping the garbage. Getting into bad moods changing diapers . . ." Winnie could feel her smile slowly fade away as she realized how much her life was going to change.

Josh got up and slipped into the seat next to Winnie's. "Having a baby is going to be hard, Win. It's going to be an even bigger challenge than being married. We're going to do our best. And we're going to make it."

"I guess that's all we can hope for," Winnie whispered, before she closed her eyes and leaned her head wearily onto Josh's shoulder.

# Eighteen

**M**elissa gripped the two steel handles of the arm curl machine, settled the backs of her upper arms into the pads, and pulled. She watched with satisfaction as her powerful biceps tightened and swelled. Then she glanced over at a track teammate on the next weight machine, straining to pull less than half the weight Melissa was managing easily.

"Whew, Melissa," the girl said with admiration, sitting back and patting her forehead with a white workout towel. "You're in great shape. How do you do it?"

"Practice." Melissa gave her a smile, tossed her

head, and pulled the arm curl up again. "Practice and the will to win."

The other girl shook her head. "Hey. I'll be out there rooting for you tomorrow, Melissa. With arms like that, you're going to be pumping. You deserve to win. You've worked hard for it."

Melissa smiled and wiped the back of her bare, sweaty neck. Tomorrow was a major regional meet on the U. of S. campus. She'd be competing in the two hundred, four hundred and eight hundred meter events. And she was planning to break all of her personal records.

There was no way she wouldn't. After all, she was feeling stronger by the day on the weights and more aggressive than ever out on the track.

Plus, she and her closest competitor, junior Caitlin Bruneau, had been working out three times a day to get ready. In the last few weeks, Caitlin had become her best friend. Caitlin had been the one who challenged her. Caitlin had been the one who made her believe in herself again. And, of course, Caitlin had introduced her to the magical cure that made it all possible.

Melissa smiled to herself as she finished the arm workout with ease. The day before, they'd even taken a trip downtown for haircuts, joking about how it would lighten them up and shave a few milliseconds off their times. Melissa's nearly shorn head was cool now, and she loved it. No more useless fussing over her appearance. In and out of the shower in a matter of seconds. What difference did it make how she looked? The important thing was winning.

Winning was everything to her now. After all, she'd learned the hard way that it was the only thing she could count on. Everything else had let her down. First it was her alcoholic father and her weak-willed mother. Then it was Brooks, who'd practically forced her to fall in love with him, only to dump her at the altar. Then it was Lauren, who had pretended to be her friend, but who only wanted to get rid of her once they got close.

"Lookin' good," Melissa heard a deep voice behind her. It was Terry Meeham, her track coach, standing with his arms crossed and his clipboard clamped to his chest. "I'm pegging you to win the eight hundred on Saturday, Melissa. You're the fastest thing out there."

"You bet." Melissa leaned down from the waist and stretched her hamstrings, grinning. "I'm ready for it."

Terry frowned a little. "You look it. Take a break, though. Don't push it. I want you healthy."

"Never felt better in my life," Melissa replied, standing up and stretching her long arms up.

"Put on a little weight?" Terry asked, narrowing his eyes curiously and looking up and down Melissa's lean, strong body.

Melissa shrugged. "A few pounds. Must be my extra workouts."

"Mmm-hmmm." Terry nodded. "Like I said, McDormand. I want you to kick back a little in the next twenty-four hours. You push yourself too hard and you'll wind up in the clinic."

"Okay, coach!"

Melissa gave Terry a sardonic grin as he ambled out of the U. of S. weight room, checking out other team members and urging them on. "Kick back," Melissa muttered to herself, walking over to the leg press and swinging her leg over the seat. "I'm about as ready to kick back as a cat in a mouse cage. I'm ready to go. I'm out for blood. And I'm going to win."

A few moments later, Caitlin strode through the weight room and gave Melissa a thumbs-up sign. With her short haircut, wide neck, and huge muscles, Caitlin looked like she could take on members of the men's track team.

"Hey." Melissa nodded.

"Hey," Caitlin answered, whispering and pointing to her workout bag. Her eyes darted nervously around the room. "You ready for the magical cure?"

Melissa looked around, too, getting up lightly from the weight machine and grabbing her gym bag. "You bet. I'm outta here."

"Looking good," Caitlin grunted. "I still think I'm going to take you in the eight hundred, though."

"No way," Melissa replied, slinging her gym bag over one powerful shoulder as they headed down the hall. Melissa looked back to see if anyone was following. But everything was quiet.

Caitlin gave her a tough grin. "Sometimes I wonder if I should have kept the magic potion all to myself. It'd be a lot easier for me if I did."

"You'd be bored silly," Melissa noted. Suddenly, the two of them stopped, looked casually up and down the hallway, then pushed open a door and ducked inside. "You'd blow everyone away and there'd be no one to compete with. No one to push you harder out there."

"Does Terry know where you are?" Caitlin asked nervously.

"Nah." Melissa shook her head. "He left the weight room a few minutes ago."

Caitlin unzipped her bag and carefully drew out several plastic bags filled with small pharmaceutical bottles, syringes, gauze, and alcohol. "Okay. Here's a little help for you. And a little help for me."

Melissa took the plastic bag and sighed with satisfaction. "Thanks again."

"What are friends for?" Caitlin shrugged, pulling out one of the tiny bottles filled with clear liquid. She unwrapped the sterile wrapper around one of the syringes and held it up in the air. Then she took one of the small bottles, stabbed the needle into it, and slowly drew the liquid from the bottle into the syringe.

"Ready, Mel?" Caitlin stared at the syringe.

"Ready," Melissa said. She turned around and lowered the top of her track shorts. She looked over her shoulder as Caitlin jabbed the shiny needle point into her lower hip and slowly pushed the liquid into her muscle.

"Done," Caitlin muttered, placing the used syringe and bottle in another bag and closing it. After dabbing Melissa's puncture with alcohol, she threw the pad into a bag and turned around herself. Melissa, meanwhile, was preparing a second syringe to give to Caitlin. "Is that door locked?"

Melissa shrugged. "Sure it is. Ridiculous, isn't it? The way we have to sneak around like this—just to get ourselves in shape."

"I know." Caitlin shook her head in disgust. "Everyone will be yelling and screaming and congratulating us tomorrow when we win. But they're not even willing to help us do what it takes."

Melissa nodded in agreement. "I don't see why people think steroids are so bad for you. I've never felt better in my life."

# Nineteen

......................................

*L*auren hung her head. Walking across the green toward Plotsky Fountain, she could barely enjoy the bright sunshine that was soaking into the damp grass. After last night's thunderstorm, everything looked fresh and new and bright.

Inside she felt tired and defeated.

I still can't believe last night, Lauren thought miserably. I can't believe I actually broke into Faith's room, then beat up her roommate. How could I have forgotten about Becker? Faith will probably never speak to me again.

Still, Lauren knew, she couldn't just mope around. She had to take action.

She already had a plan.

She sat down under a large oak tree across from the fountain and waited. It was three o'clock and everyone she'd called last night had promised to come.

Brooks.

Winnie.

Even KC. And Josh.

Last night, in all of the confusion and noise of Faith's room, Lauren realized something. She could see in her friend's exhausted face that she wasn't the only one who was leaning on Faith too hard. Everyone was.

Faith was kind and generous and giving. And now everyone had started taking her for granted. They had used her as their personal sounding board and counselor—without thinking about what they could give back.

And now Faith was really cracking up.

"Over here, Win!" Lauren shouted across the dorm green when she saw Winnie's neon-orange bodysuit emerge from her French class.

Lauren played with a blade of grass between her fingers, and thought back to last fall, when she and Faith were roommates. Faith had been the one who'd helped her through her first few months of paralyzing insecurity. Through Faith, she'd met most of her closest friends.

A few minutes later Brooks appeared and plopped

down on the grass. Josh arrived, walking and reading a software manual at the same time. KC and her boyfriend, Cody Wainwright, sat on the grass with their arms around each other, gazing into each other's eyes.

"Thanks for coming, you guys," Lauren said wearily.

"No problem," Brooks said, gruffly clearing his throat.

"Like I said on the phone last night," Lauren began, "we've got to do something. We've all been asking too much of Faith, and now I'm afraid we're going to lose her. She's really, really angry. She practically told me she never wanted to see me or any of her friends again. And that means all of us."

"It's that awful Becker Cain's influence." Winnie glared into the distance. "Possibly the most obnoxious human being within a fifty-mile radius."

"Very superior." Lauren nodded. "But I do think she likes him."

Winnie looked stunned. "No way."

Brooks was nodding. "Yeah. Good old Mr. Cool and Philosophical."

"Ugh," Winnie groaned. "With his creepy black clothes and that stupid question-mark button he wears on his lapel."

Brooks nodded. "Yeah. As if he actually wanted us to come up to him and say, 'Gee, Becker, here's the answer. What's the question?'"

Lauren straightened up. "But we're not here to talk about Becker. We're here for Faith."

Winnie sagged down onto the grass. "I feel terrible about what's happened," she moaned. "I'm probably the guiltiest one of all. I dragged her down to the bus station yesterday when she had a million other things to do. It's just that Faith has always been there for me. It's second nature for me to include her in my problems."

KC looked around at the group. "I haven't seen Faith all week. I've been a real stranger. So now I feel guilty. I should have checked in with her to see if she needed anything. But . . ."

Lauren nodded. "But she never seems to need anything. That's the thing about Faith. She's a giver. It's not her nature to ask for help."

Winnie flopped back on the grass. "I think I make up for her. I don't hesitate. I don't even think. I just get right in there and mindlessly grab all the help I think my greedy little self deserves."

Josh looked up, confused. "Win," he protested briefly, before sinking his head back down in his manual.

KC reached over and patted Winnie's head. "You're a giver too, Win. You've been there for me through high school and now here. I've been the selfish one . . ."

"No," Winnie shook her head. "I've definitely been more selfish. Much, much more."

"I'm the worst. I can't believe the way I dragged

her downtown the night before last," Brooks said miserably. "She told me she had a big thing coming up, but s-somehow . . ." he stammered. "I don't know. I guess old habits are hard to break." He looked up. "So what's up, Lauren?"

Lauren took a deep breath. "Well," she said, "we all know we've been taking advantage of her. She had the Western Civ exam, her big theater presentation, and the Coed-by-Bed thing to complicate her life. What a week. And we made it harder for her. I think it's time we told her we were sorry. Let's try to make it up to her."

"Poor Faith," KC whispered.

"Agreed?" Lauren looked around the group.

Everyone nodded.

"Okay," Lauren murmured. "She's giving her theater presentation right now and should be headed this way when she's done. So let's wait."

Everyone settled down.

"Hey." Winnie rubbed her hands together. "Let's throw her a big party over at our house. We'll make a big banner that tells her how much she is loved. We'll really surprise her."

"Do we need to do all that?" KC wondered, curling a lock of Cody's hair around her forefinger. "Maybe we just need to apologize. Maybe we just need to tell her that we get the message. And that if she needs our help, we're here."

"Let's do both," Lauren said firmly. "Deal?"

"Deal," the group said in a chorus.

"Now all we have to do is wait." KC sighed.

"Yeah," Winnie added. "Wait and decide if we should invite that awful Becker to the party."

"How does Faith stand him?" KC asked with a curious look. "He's too perfect. He sounds exactly like the sort of guy Faith can't stand."

"Faith Crowley?" The voice of the drama department chairman boomed through the dark theater.

Faith breathed in slowly, then exhaled. She stood up and rolled her neck. Then she took a slow sip of coffee, trying to blot out the image of last night's chaotic scene in her dorm room.

"Faith Crowley?"

"Yes," Faith called out calmly. "I'm ready." Setting down her cup, Faith stood up and made her way serenely down the aisle and up the steps to the University Theater's main stage. Continuing to take deep breaths, Faith was trying to imagine she was sailing on a tranquil sea, as Becker had suggested. She tried to visualize her Shrew proposal being approved and her life finally on track.

But little ghosts kept popping up in her head.

Brooks.

Lauren.

Winnie.

No! She couldn't think about them. This was her moment. She had to focus. Everything depended on that now!

Faith took her seat on a stool and faced the line of drama department faculty members seated before her. *If it hadn't been for Becker, I'd be a basket case,* she thought.

But Becker had been there for her. He had laid his amazing wild West *Shrew* concept right in her lap. He had brought her coffee in the morning. Then had helped her meditate and relax.

"Are you ready, Faith?" she heard the drama department head asking wearily. They had been listening to production proposals for several hours now and many were already shifting in their seats and puffing restlessly on cigarettes. Out of fifty applicants for the Professional Theater Program, only fifteen would be selected.

"Yes, I am," Faith replied, folding her hands in her lap. The idea for Shrew was so fresh and settled in her mind, she knew she wouldn't even have to refer to her notes. Talking about it would be like having a clear, sparkling stream flowing from her brain to her lips. Because she knew the idea was exactly right.

"Go ahead, then."

"My entrance exam assignment has been to develop a fresh production approach to Taming of the

Shrew," Faith began clearly, staring fearlessly into the eyes of the faculty members. "My concept begins by placing the performance in a wild West setting—a choice that not only allows for playfulness and movement on stage, but which also will underscore the violent, dueling nature of the relationship between Petruchio and Katharina."

Faith watched calmly as the faculty members nodded with approval and made notes.

"I envision the set as a lively western barroom, complete with chorus girls, fiddle music, and sparring cowboys," Faith went on. "Katharina is the brainy girl-outlaw who finally meets her match in Petruchio and who refuses to accept a subordinate role to him, even though she pretends to in the end."

Faith gazed out at the faculty members, who had stopped fidgeting and now looked visibly impressed with her presentation.

"Katharina's need to find a man who is her equal, yet who can love her womanly side, may be played with humor." Faith crossed her legs and leaned forward with conviction. "Perhaps her lacy petticoat only thinly disguises the rough-looking pair of leather chaps she wears underneath."

There were a few chuckles and a murmur of approval from the audience.

"Perhaps Petruchio and Katharina's conversations always take place at gunpoint," Faith continued, "and it's only when they put their guns back in their holsters that they truly come together . . ."

"Ha!" One of the drama professors clapped with delight. "Marvelous!"

A wave of white-hot energy zapped through Faith's body. The time she'd spent back in high school memorizing long passages from Shrew was now paying off. This was it. This is what she wanted to do with her life. Her future wasn't a far-off dream anymore. Her future was right here in the theater. Telling stories. Listening to language and making a hundred different talents all come together for a few rare moments of magic.

"Uh . . . excuse me, Miss Crowley," Faith's stagecraft instructor spoke up. "How would you handle the limitations of such a specific set in this play? Wouldn't a barroom create obstacles for you in the production?"

"No, I don't think so," Faith began earnestly, feeling like she could go head-to-head with William Shakespeare if she had to. Eagerly she explained the way her set could adapt to the text. Bar stools became trees. Mirrors became the sun. Chandeliers became stars. Everything she'd ever learned was all coming together in this moment.

When Faith's presentation was finally over, she felt as if she'd run a marathon—and won.

"Thank you, Faith," the department chairman

called out, leaning over and murmuring something to his colleagues.

"Thank you," Faith murmured, standing up and starting to leave the stage.

"Uh . . . just a minute, Faith. Hang on," the chairman called out.

Faith stopped in the middle of the stage and looked curiously down at him. Holding her notebook lightly to her side, she strolled back to the stool and quietly sat down while the faculty members continued to talk among themselves and nod.

"Faith," the chairman called out again. "We don't see any reason to keep you waiting. Your presentation was as excellent as your resume and references. It was original, theatrical, and very well thought out. We'd like to accept you into our program right now."

Faith gasped and drew a hand up to her mouth. "I'm in?"

There was friendly laughter from among the faculty members. "You are definitely in, Faith. It's unanimous," the faculty chairman insisted. "The Professional Theater Program is generally reserved for upper-division and graduate students at this university. But you have a high level of creativity and a solid record of ability. There's no question that both you and the Program will benefit if we start you right away."

"Thank you," Faith said in a rush. She stood up, not

knowing what else to say. "Really. Thank you. It . . . it means a lot to me."

It took all of Faith's self-control to keep from dashing up the aisle screaming at the top of her lungs. Instead, she smiled, waved politely, and headed toward the door into the lobby, thinking only of Becker and how she had to find him right away.

Outside, the warm sunshine on her bare arms had never felt so good. She was exhausted, but her body felt light and her mind was suddenly free.

I'm in! Thanks to Becker and thanks to me, I'm in! Faith thought with joy, turning down the path toward Coleridge Hall. She balled her hands up into fists and beat the air. Her so-called friends had tried to distract her and create obstacles, but she'd made it anyway. Becker had been there for her. And she'd never be able to thank him enough.

"Faith!" She heard someone calling her from the dorm green. She winced inwardly, recognizing Winnie's high-pitched voice. Then she looked over and recoiled in horror. There, about fifty yards away from her, was not only Winnie but Brooks and Lauren and KC and Josh.

Faith just stood there for a moment, staring in disbelief.

"Faith!" Lauren screamed. "We need to talk to you!"

Faith didn't stop to hear more. She turned immediately on her heels and broke into a light jog. She was through being badgered and manipulated. Her friends weren't going to abuse her good nature anymore. After all, who did they think she was?

Clutching her notebook, Faith sped past Mill Pond, her braid flying and her legs pumping. As she neared her dorm, her jog had turned into occasional leaping. Her smile had turned into an ecstatic grin. She was in the Program. And she owed it all to the one person who had believed in her and respected her dream.

Chugging up the stairway, Faith stuffed her hand in her jean pocket and pulled out her key. But when she pushed open the door, she realized that she didn't need it. Because Becker was there, waiting for her.

"I made it!" Faith screamed, running up behind him and grabbing him around the waist. "I'm in the program. We did it!"

"What?" Becker twisted around, still in her arms. His pale blue eyes had opened wide and his long, handsome face had broken out into a look of stunned happiness. "They told you already?"

"Yes!" Faith began playfully pummeling his strong chest. "The presentation went really well. They loved the idea. And I was calm enough to actually think. It was perfect." Faith grabbed both of his hands and began jumping up and down. Then she flung her arms around his neck and kissed him.

"You're perfect," Becker whispered, drawing away for a moment before he kissed her back. He took her hand and broke out into a wide smile, pulling her down on the bed. "I'm really happy for you, Faith. You deserve it."

"It was your idea," Faith breathed, toppling over next to his long body and staring absently at the neat piles of clothes all around them.

Becker snaked his arm around her waist, sending little shivers of delight and warmth through her body. She wanted to fall inside his eyes and make his arm stay where it was forever. "But don't you see?" Becker murmured. "I just gave you the seed of an idea. You ran with it. You knew the text. It was your dream—and you made it happen."

"People have dreams," Faith whispered, slipping her fingers through his long hair, "but they can't always get there alone. I couldn't have. You were the only one who could have helped me. And some-how—magically—you happened to be the one who walked through that door four days ago."

Becker smiled back and drew her close. Then they kissed. This time, longer and deeper than ever before. But Faith was ready.

After a few moments, Faith opened her eyes and looked at him seriously. "You were right about my old friends."

"I was?" Becker had narrowed his dark eyebrows

and was looking at her with his usual mix of interest and sympathy.

"They just don't care about me, Becker," Faith said firmly, though she felt lost and sad as she said the words. "It hasn't been easy for me. You have to understand. These are people I've known for years. People I always thought truly cared about me. But they nearly cost me the thing I wanted most in life right now."

Becker was nodding quietly and Faith could almost see her own sadness reflected back in his eyes.

Tears were beginning to slip down Faith's cheeks. "It hurts, Becker. It really hurts."

After a few moments she sat up and looked around. Becker had removed his clothes from his drawer and had folded them next to his black duffel. His books, pens, and notebooks were piled neatly on the desk. "What's all this?" Faith wanted to know. "You're not supposed to leave until Sunday morning. It's only Friday afternoon."

Becker stood up and walked away from her toward the window. His hair fell down over the collar of his plain T-shirt and his hands were stuffed into the pockets of his black pants. "Faith," he began in a somber tone.

Faith froze. Why was he beginning to sound so icy? For a split second, she panicked. Was Becker going to sabotage her, too? Just like the rest of her friends had? He couldn't leave now, just when she was really starting to get attached. Could he?

"The main rule of this dorm experiment was that our relationship had to remain platonic," Becker said seriously, touching the windowsill with his fingertips, his back still to her.

Faith's jaw dropped open in fear. "Yes, I know. Completely nonphysical. But . . ."

Becker turned around and smiled. "I-I just don't think I could stay here another night and remain platonic friends, Faith."

Faith was momentarily confused, until she saw that his eyes were twinkling at her.

"I have to leave now," Becker murmured, walking toward her, "because this is where our relationship begins."

"Oh, Becker," Faith cried out, getting up from the bed and walking shyly toward him.

Becker held Faith with his large, warm hands. "No more experiments. No more closing our eyes. No more tame gestures and meaningful looks. I want you, Faith. We belong together.

Faith could barely speak, she was so relieved and overwhelmed at the same time.

"It's time for us to move on to something much more important, Faith," Becker whispered. "Much more important."

*Here's a sneak preview of*
**Freshman Obsession,** *the twenty-fourth book in the FRESHMAN DORM series.*

O utside, the air was cool, but Melissa was sweating. Her anger was so great, so explosive, so hot, she felt like the top of her head might blow off and go clattering across the pavement like a manhole cover after a steam pipe explosion.

She'd just dumped a whole box of stuff belonging to Brooks in front of his dorm room door. That included the quilt he'd given her as a conciliatory gift. What incredible nerve he had! Nothing could make up for the fact that he'd gotten cold feet at the altar. Nothing could make up for the humiliation and shabby treatment he'd subjected her to.

Melissa felt sick at the memory of it all, but exhilarated as she thought of Brooks and mentally rehearsed the scathing things she would say to him if she ever got him cornered.

Suddenly she realized that the hair on her arms was standing. She had that "somebody is watching me" feeling again.

*I'm getting paranoid,* she thought, looking quickly around.

But across the quad, she saw a familiar face. A guy with deep green eyes lifted a gloved hand and gave her a tentative wave.

Automatically, Melissa's hand rose and fluttered in his direction.

The guy began to wheel his chair in her direction.

Melissa felt like kicking herself. Why had she waved? She didn't want to talk to him. She didn't want to talk to anybody right now.

But he seemed eager to speak with her. As his chair got closer, his smile grew broader. "Hello!" he said. "At last, we meet again."

"Hi." Melissa nodded curtly.

He extended his hand to shake. "We were never formally introduced. I'm Daniel Markham. My friends call me Danny."

Melissa tried to smile.

"Is that the best you can do?"

"What do you mean?"

"I mean I've seen happier faces in coffins."

"You've probably seen happier people in coffins," she muttered, kicking the toe of her running shoe against the curb.

"Whoaaa! That's some mood you're in. What's the matter? The leg bothering you again? I notice you're still favoring the left leg."

Melissa bristled. "You're crazy," she bluffed. "My leg is fine."

"Oh, yeah. Right," he said sarcastically. "Mine too. There's not a whole lot I can do for mine, though. What are you doing for yours?"

"I'm resting it," she admitted grudgingly. "Not that it's any of your business. And not that there's anything wrong with it."

He chuckled and shrugged. "If that's your story, stick to it. I'm not your coach. But if I were your coach, I'd be concerned about that leg—along with a couple of other things."

"What *other things*?"

"Let me put it this way: If I were a coach and I saw one of my star runners spending a lot of time with the body builders, I'd take that runner aside and have a serious heart-to-heart."

"What are you implying?"

He smiled genially. "I'm not *implying* anything. I'll spell it out for you if you want." Danny squinted, studying her face. "Is it my imagination, or are your eyes beginning to look a little yellow?"

Melissa's face began to grow pale. She knew exactly what he meant. He was talking about the steroids. Well, let him speculate. He didn't know anything for a fact. Couldn't prove anything. And he wasn't her coach.

"What have you got against body builders?" she demanded, deciding that the best defense was a good offense. "I've seen you in the gym."

"Sure. I work the weights. But I stay natural. And to answer your question, I've got nothing against body builders. But some of those guys are fooling themselves in a very dangerous way. Steroids are just another form of substance abuse. They're doing big time damage to their bodies. And when I see people purposefully hurting themselves, it makes me angry."

Melissa turned on her heels and began to walk away.

"Hey!" she heard him shout behind her.

Melissa kept walking.

*"HOLD IT!"*

She turned.

"I just want to know one thing."

Melissa waited.

"What the hell have *you* got to be so angry about?" Danny wheeled the chair quickly over to where she stood and looked up at her. "What's got you so chafed?"

"You wouldn't understand."

"Wouldn't understand what? Wouldn't understand the pressures of competition? Wouldn't understand the desire for perfection? Wouldn't understand the feeling that your whole life rides on the results of a race? Believe me, I understand. I was an athlete once."

"Track?"

"Football."

"So you weren't always in the—" she broke off awkwardly.

" . . . always in the wheelchair?" he finished for her. "No. I wasn't born with a wheelchair stuck under my butt."

Melissa began to turn red.

"You don't have to be embarrassed. It's a wheelchair. I'm not naked."

She choked back a laugh. "Look. I don't really have time to talk right now but—"

"Fine. Then *I'll* talk. I'll tell you the story of my life so that the next time I run into you, you won't be scared to talk to me because you're afraid of saying something tactless."

"I'm not scared to talk to you," Melissa retorted.

"Right!" he said sarcastically. "You probably talk to people in wheelchairs every day. So anyway. Where was I? Oh yeah. It was a dark and stormy night, and Daniel Markham had just scored three touchdowns in the final game of the season that afternoon. The football scholarship was in the bag and Markham decided to celebrate. He didn't use drugs. Drugs were for junkies. Daniel Markham didn't need drugs to feel powerful and invincible. He felt powerful and invincible already. So powerful and invincible that, after the game, he thought he could gulp down a fifth of vodka and drive his car into a tree going sixty miles an hour and not get hurt. And you know what?"

He adjusted one of his fingerless leather gloves and shook the hair off his shoulders.

"Turned out I wasn't Superman after all. Nobody is that powerful. And nobody is that invincible. I severed my spinal cord, spent a year in a hospital and rehabilitation center and wound up sitting here in a wheelchair trying to tell a pretty girl that substance abuse is substance abuse is substance abuse."

He waggled his eyebrows and dropped his voice in a coy aside. "And you thought this story wouldn't have a moral."

Melissa glared at him. *"Leave me alone!"* she shouted.

"No," he said pleasantly. "I don't think I will."